Janine Lewis

The Girl at the Hostel

novum pro

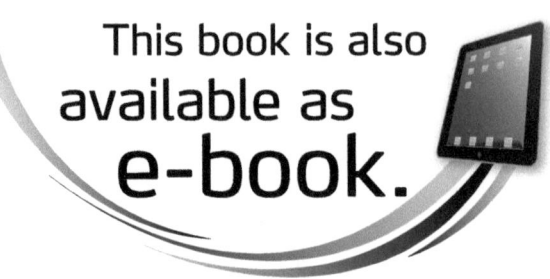

This book is also
available as
e-book.

www.novum-publishing.co.uk

© 2023 novum publishing

ISBN 978-3-99131-322-9
Editing: Charlotte Middleton
Cover photos: Place4design, Razihusin,
Dvdeo I Dreamstime.com
Cover design, layout & typesetting:
novum publishing

www.novum-publishing.co.uk

Climate neutral
Print product
ClimatePartner.com/16547-2201-1002

Contents

Chapter 1

On a cold winter evening in Leeds city centre, people rushed up and down the streets. Some were on their way home, others on their way to work, and others were going out for the night. It was one week until Christmas – all the lights were on and you could feel the buzz of excitement in the air. One person who could not feel any excitement at that moment in time though was Morgan.

Thirteen-year-old Morgan had been homeless for three months. On this particular night, she had managed to find a shop doorway to snuggle up in and had collected enough money in her cup to buy a sandwich and a cup of tea. Sitting in her sleeping bag, she quickly sipped her tea and ate the sandwich as passers-by made their way up or down the street, some looking at her, some acting like they couldn't see her.

Morgan had been living on the streets of Leeds city centre ever since she had had a massive row with her mum. Her mum had never really been good at picking boyfriends. And she had always tended to put her own needs before Morgan's.

Her mum was called Tasmin and the most recent boyfriend was Greg. Morgan had had a funny feeling about him from the first time she had seen him. He had thin, pursed lips, a jutting jaw and cruel eyes. Whenever Tasmin was around, he would act nice, but as soon as she left the room, he would slide his hand up Morgan's leg and touch her in a way that made her feel very uncomfortable.

The abuse went on for months. Then, one day, Morgan decided enough was enough. She had to tell her mum about the abuse.

"It's Greg," she said to her mum. "He... he keeps touching me in a harassing way and I don't think it's right, really, what he's doing. And he knows it's not right either because he told me not to tell you."

Tasmin took a drag from cigarette and said in disbelief, "You're lying. You don't want me and Greg to be happy. You're a jealous little madam."

Part of Morgan wasn't even shocked at her mum's reaction. She was constantly choosing men over her. Morgan had already been in care three times since her dad had left when she was five. She wasn't going to take this lying down though.

"How can you take his side over me?" Morgan asked, baffled. "I'm your daughter; I should mean more to you than any man."

Then, the living room door opened and Greg came in. "Everything all right, love?" he said to Tasmin, kissing her on the cheek.

"No, not really," she fumed, glaring at Morgan.

"What's wrong?" he asked, looking from Tasmin to Morgan.

"You'll never guess what she's just told me," Tasmin said to him.

"What's happening in here?" Greg asked, a bit worried at this point.

There was an awkward silence. Then Tasmin said to Greg, "She said you've been harassing her. I know it's a lie though. I know you'd never do anything like that."

"Of course I wouldn't," said Greg. "Morgan, how could you make something like this up?"

"I'm not making anything up," Morgan said defensively. "You're the only one who's lying." She turned to her mum. "Why don't you believe me?"

"Because you're a liar!" Tasmin yelled. "How dare you make an accusation like this! I don't know what's wrong with you sometimes."

"There's nothing wrong with me," Morgan said, almost in tears. "But there's clearly something wrong with him. Can't you see that? He's not who you think he is, mum."

"You just want to split us up," Tasmin said, reassuring herself. "Well, it's not going to happen. Ever."

Morgan looked at Greg. His face was cold and expressionless. She looked at her mum, who looked furious. There was no convincing her.

"Right," Morgan said, and she stormed up to her room. She packed a few belongings in her rucksack, put it on her back and then came back downstairs.

"Where do you think you're going?" Tasmin asked when she saw the rucksack.

"Away from here, that's where I'm going. Anywhere's safer than here," Morgan replied.

"Well, give me your keys, then. If you're going to leave, you're not coming back here," Tasmin said nastily.

"Good! I don't want to come back here," Morgan shouted, and she gave her mum the keys. Tasmin unlocked the door and as Morgan ran out, Tasmin said, "I hope I never see you again, you liar."

"You just don't care, do you?" Morgan said to her mum. She looked at Greg. He had a very smug look on his face. She felt like slapping him.

Instead, she just said defiantly, "I'm out of here," and walked down the garden path and out of the gate, not looking back.

Walking down the road, she shivered a little. It was autumn now and it was starting to get cold. Summer had hardly seemed to last. It wasn't fair. Life wasn't fair. How could her mum choose Greg over her?

Morgan didn't really know where to go to begin with. She felt a little bit scared, but she carried on walking until she got to a bus shelter. She looked in her rucksack and got her purse out. There was still a bit of money from when she had tidied a neighbour's garden about two weeks before. After a few minutes a bus came, and she paid the fare into town.

At least it was nice and warm on the bus. There were a few other passengers. One or two had headphones in; some were reading *Metro*. They all seemed to be in their own worlds.

Morgan started to wonder if she'd done the right thing. Was she really going to survive out there? Truth be told, she didn't have a very good idea about how to make ends meet. She was still thirteen. There was no way she was going back to her mum's house though.

Then she thought of her grandma. Should she ring her and ask her if she could stay there? Actually, maybe that wasn't such a good idea. Her grandma would probably just tell her to stop being silly and to go back to her mum's.

She didn't want to ring anyone else in the family because she knew everyone had their own problems. And she hadn't seen some of them for a long time anyway. They'd probably forgotten about her.

No, she thought to herself, you've made the right decision.

She looked up as the bus slowed down. It had arrived in the city centre near the Corn Exchange. She thanked the driver as she got off the bus and looked around her. Where should she stay tonight?

Wandering the streets, she tried not to look too scared and held her head up high. Nobody even looked at her at first. She found a spot in a shop doorway and took her sleeping bag out of her rucksack. It was then that people started looking.

Putting her cup on the ground, she got in the sleeping bag and waited for people to put money in the cup. Five minutes went by. Nothing in the cup. Fifteen minutes went by. Still nothing. Half an hour later and still no-one had put any money in the cup.

Morgan bit her lip anxiously. It was starting to get dark and she felt lonely and frightened. On the other hand, she didn't want to go back to her mum's because of her horrible stepdad. Anything was better than going back there. She felt lost though. No-one cared. She was just a nobody, all alone with no-one to help her. What was she going to do?

It was now three months down the line and not much had changed for Morgan. She still had nowhere to stay or get a wash and she often felt hungry. She would reuse the same bottle and get water from the sink in a McDonald's toilets every day, so at least she had something to drink throughout the day.

To begin with, she had felt too scared and self-conscious to ask people for money. After the first couple of nights though, she realised she had to, or she would starve. Sometimes she would get up to four or five pounds in change and she would buy a sandwich and some crisps, a warm cheese-and-onion pasty from Greggs, especially now that it was getting cold.

On this particular night, she had now finished her sandwich and her cup of tea and sat there in the shop doorway, looking at the floor. It was hard being out there on her own with not a friend in the world. She had never really been good at making friends and didn't have anyone she could talk to regularly. It wasn't much use talking to other homeless people – how could they help her get out of poverty if they were in poverty themselves?

A group of about five young men walked up the street. One of them nudged one of the others, who had a drink in his hand. He whispered something in his ear.

Then the one with the drink said to Morgan, "Want a drink?" before nastily spilling it all over her.

Morgan gasped. "There was no need for that," she said, but the man and his friends just pointed at her and laughed and sneered. After a while, they walked off, still laughing horribly.

Morgan waited until they were out of sight. Then she began to cry. As the tears rolled down her beautiful face, she looked desperately up at the sky. She wished she was dead. "God help me," she whispered, and she hugged herself, the bitter wind lashing her cheeks as people passed her by on that cold night in December.

Chapter 2

Morgan Harris was born on the 9th May 1990 to an English mother, Tasmin, and a Jamaican father, Donald. She was only a baby when her father left, so she never really had any memories of him. She didn't even have a photo of him. All she really knew about him was that he used to work in a bar and that was how he met her mother.

When Morgan was growing up, several men walked in and out of her mother's life. Morgan lost count of the number of boyfriends her mum had had over the years. Morgan never really got on with any of them because they thought they could boss her about and that they were her dad when they clearly weren't.

The Harris's had moved house several times throughout Morgan's childhood. Morgan had been to six different primary schools and two different high schools. This meant that she had never really had the chance to make lasting friendships. She had only made two friends in her whole school life – one when she was five and another when she was eight – but because she always moving schools, she had lost contact with them.

Because she hardly ever had any friends, she was often an easy target for bullies. The bullying became a real problem at her second high school. All the other kids in her year had already made friends and she was the odd one out. Sometimes the abuse was verbal, sometimes even physical. They would follow her around the school and bump into her on purpose and pull her hair. Once, three girls ganged up on her after school, beat her up and stole her money so she couldn't get the bus. She had to walk home, which was several miles from the school. When she finally got there, her mum just gave her a funny look.

"What's happened to you?" she asked when she saw Morgan's black eye.

"These girls got me after school."

"Serves you right. You're always going around on your own. You should make some friends. Why don't you have any friends? What's wrong with you?"

"What do you mean? It isn't my fault no-one wants to be my friend, is it?" Morgan protested.

"Shut up, whingeing. Go upstairs and get changed. Dinner will be ready soon."

Typical, Morgan thought to herself and went to her own room.

That day always stuck in her mind. Not so much because of the attack. More because her mum had shown very little concern. She just didn't care.

Morgan was scared of being beaten up again, so she started skipping school. She didn't want to be targeted and didn't care very much for school anyway. She couldn't tell a teacher that she had been bullied because they wouldn't understand. They never did. And they never listened to anything she had to say, those teachers. She felt alienated and like she didn't fit in. There was just no point in going any more.

She was about twelve when she started skipping school. She would usually just go into town and wander round the shops, have some chips for lunch, then get the bus and go to the park or something. She would find a bench, plonk herself down, then wonder why no-one in this world cared about her. Was it her fault? Should she try harder to make friends? Or were the other kids at school just cruel and nasty?

One day, Tasmin got a call from the headteacher of Morgan's school.

"I think you have a right to know that your daughter hasn't been attending school," he said.

"Oh my goodness," Tasmin squealed with fake concern. "I didn't even realise. I have been sending her to school."

"What are you going to do about this, Miss Harris?" the headteacher asked.

"She'll get a good telling off, don't you worry. And she'll be back at school on Monday. Even if I have to drag her there."

"Okay, Mrs Harris," the headteacher said, not sounding too convinced. What could he do though? Morgan wasn't his child. She wasn't his responsibility. He simply said, "Goodbye," to Morgan's mother and got on with his day. It wasn't his worry.

When Morgan got home, Tasmin was sat in the kitchen smoking a cigarette. She heard Morgan trying to go up the stairs.

"Not so fast," she said inhaling. "You come in the kitchen."

Morgan reluctantly obeyed. As she came in, her mother sat there at the table, exhaling and surveying Morgan with watchful blue eyes.

"What's this I hear about you bunking off school?" she asked Morgan. She had to ask her, at least.

There was an extremely long pause. Then Morgan said, "I just don't like it, Mum. They leave me out all the time and it's just no fun."

Her mum watched her. Then she asked in an offhand voice, which hinted that she wasn't really bothered either way, "So, are you going back on Monday then?"

"I don't want to," Morgan said, folding her arms stubbornly.

Tasmin put her cigarette out, exhaling. Then she looked at her daughter and said rather carelessly, "Well, it's your choice, isn't it?"

Morgan was speechless. She was surprised that her mother wasn't that angry. She also felt a bit hurt because she had thought her mum would be more concerned about her welfare and education. But her mum hardly seemed to care about anything but herself.

Tasmin had got herself a new boyfriend. His name was Greg. Morgan didn't like him. She hadn't really liked any of her mum's boyfriends, but there was something particularly creepy about this one.

Just as the little conversation finished, he came through the front door. "Hello, love," he said to Tasmin. Then he looked at Morgan.

"I don't know what you're looking at," Morgan said stroppily. She didn't like the way he looked at her. He watched her in a leering way which made her feel uncomfortable.

"Don't you give my Greg any lip!" Tasmin squealed.

Morgan tutted and rolled her eyes. "Hello, Morgan," Greg finally said, widening his eyes. "And how's your day been?" he said, trying to sound pleasant.

Morgan didn't answer. She left the kitchen and went up to her room. "Kids," she heard Greg mutter as she went upstairs. "Who'd have 'em?"

In her room, Morgan sat on her bed and tried to look on the bright side of things. At least she didn't have to go to that school anymore, because her mum didn't care either way. However, the fact that her mum didn't care also meant that she probably wouldn't enrol her in a new school. Morgan would have nowhere to go; she would just be on the streets or stuck at home. It wasn't ideal.

A thought suddenly came into her head. She thought of leaving home. If she did that though, she would need a job, an income, and it was difficult for people of her age to find jobs. She groaned and hugged her pillow as she wondered what she was going to do with her life.

It was 9th May 2003, the day of Morgan's thirteenth birthday. She could hardly sleep the night before, she was so excited. When she woke up and realised she was now a teenager, she jumped out of bed and drew the curtains.

The sun was shining so brightly. The warm rays fell onto Morgan's freckled brown skin and she smiled. After it had sunk in that she wasn't twelve any more, she went into the bathroom to have a shower and then got dressed in her favourite jumper and a denim skirt and boots. Flying down the stairs, she could hardly contain her joy.

The joy would not last very long, though. Morgan was extremely disappointed when she discovered that the only thing her mum had bought her was a pair of socks. She tried hard to hide the disappointment, but it must have showed, because her mum frowned at her.

"Don't you be so ungrateful," Tasmin snapped at her daughter. "Some people don't get any presents on their birthday."

"A pair of socks? I should be grateful for a crappy pair of socks?" Morgan moaned.

"Yes! They're from Marks and Spencer, those," Tasmin told her, as if that was supposed to make them an extra special pair of socks.

"I don't care where you got them; I think I deserve more than that. You did the same thing at Christmas as well."

"Well," Greg chipped in, although it was clearly none of his business, "you could start a sock collection, couldn't you?" His voice was quite patronising, and Morgan looked him up and down.

"I never asked for your opinion," Morgan said in the teenager fashion.

"Right, that's it," Tasmin said. "Go back upstairs. I've told you before to watch how you talk to my Greg," she went on, while Greg stood there giving Morgan a nasty smirk behind Tasmin's back.

"Don't really care, anyway," Morgan said, her arms folded. She turned and went up to her room.

The rest of the day was quite painful for Morgan. There was no sign that she was having her thirteenth birthday – there was no music, no cake, no nothing. While her mum and Greg sat in the kitchen talking about goodness knows what, Morgan thought that there must be some way to celebrate. She came out of her room and went into the living room.

Then, she noticed her mum's handbag on the armchair. She took a cigarette out of her mum's bag and then checked that no-one was coming out of the kitchen. The coast was clear, so she went out of the front door, which was almost always unlocked, and walked to the local park.

Sitting on a swing, she got the matchbox she had bought from the corner shop, took a match out and lit the cigarette. She took a drag, then inhaled more deeply as she smoked the whole cigarette bit by bit. It felt fantastic. Her life was far from fantastic at the moment though. Actually, she didn't think her life could get any worse.

Christmas Eve had come and there was some good news for Morgan. She had recently met another homeless person called Taylor, who had told her about a place that they could stay that night and tomorrow. It was called Shield, and it was only about half a mile away from the city centre. So, before it got dark, they set off to find this shelter they so badly needed.

Taylor was older than Morgan. She told Morgan that she had become homeless because she couldn't afford to pay her rent anymore and was subsequently evicted from her flat. Morgan listened intently as they walked. It was nice to have someone to talk to, someone in the same situation as her.

When they got to Shield, they looked at each other.

"Well, this is it," said Taylor, and she knocked on the door. A man opened it. He had dark brown hair and wore trendy thick-rimmed glasses, a burgundy jumper with a picture of a Christmas pudding on it, jeans, trainers and a Santa hat on his head.

"Hello!" he said cheerfully. "How can I help you two young ladies?"

"We just wondered if we could stay the night," Taylor said, trying not to sound too desperate or too scared either. "We're sleeping rough, you see, and we heard about Shield and what you do and we – er..." Taylor was running out of things to say.

"Well, no-one wants to be on the streets at Christmas, do they?" Morgan added. Taylor nudged her but the man didn't seem to mind.

"Of course you can stay," he said warmly. "Mind you, it's only for tonight and tomorrow, then you have to go."

"That's fine, absolutely fine," Taylor said, grinning gratefully. The man, whose name turned out to be John, held the door open for them and they stepped inside.

Taylor took her hat off and tossed her mousey brown hair. Morgan looked around. She went to what she assumed was the living room and poked her head round the door. Several gaunt faces looked back to her. She turned to John.

"So, when's dinner?" she asked.

"Morgan!" Taylor exclaimed. "We've only just got here."

John just chuckled. "We'll start serving dinner at about five thirty p.m. I'll take you two up to your room first though."

The room was wonderfully spacious, with two beds, a radio and a beautiful view of the city. As soon as John started going back downstairs, Taylor got on one of the beds and started jumping up and down. Morgan switched the radio on. It was playing Christmas songs like The Pogues and Slade and Mariah Carey.

Morgan had to sing along when Mariah Carey's "All I Want For Christmas is You" came on: that was her favourite. She and Taylor danced around and then had a pillow fight. When the radio DJ announced that it was coming up to five thirty p.m., they rushed downstairs for dinner.

There were eight of them altogether – three female, five male. The other girl barely spoke or made eye contact with anyone. She had the name "Brian" tattooed on her neck and wore a light blue dress not really suitable for the cold winter. She was stick thin and had delicate features. The guys wouldn't stop looking at her.

Dinner turned out to be tomato soup and French bread with butter. The soup was thick and creamy. Morgan said, "Mmm," as it ran down her throat, warming her up. The bread was crusty on the outside and soft and chewy on the inside. When she finished, she wanted more but thought it would be a bit greedy of her to ask for more.

In the living room afterward, they all shared a box of Celebrations. Then John put the stereo on and they all danced. The girl with the tattoo on her neck and one of guys kept kissing and couldn't keep their hands off each other. Morgan made a vomiting noise.

The tattooed girl stopped kissing the guy and said, "Who was that?"

Taylor pointed to Morgan.

"If you don't bloody like it, don't look," the tattooed girl said to Morgan in a hostile voice. Then she and the guy carried on kissing.

Morgan spent about ten more minutes at the party then snuck out and went upstairs. Taylor came up about an hour after Morgan.

"Why did you leave the party so early?" she asked Morgan.

"Why do you think?" Morgan said in a sulky voice, then she pulled the duvet over her head.

"Was it because of that girl?"

There was a pause. "No, it was the whole group really," Morgan said, pulling the duvet off her face. "They're not really like us, are they?"

"Don't know what you're talking about, love," Taylor said flippantly.

"All right, then," Morgan said a bit sadly.

"Goodnight."

"Night."

When Christmas morning came, Morgan woke up before Taylor. She drew the curtains. It was snowing a little bit but not enough to completely cover the ground and the rooftops. Morgan felt an overwhelming sense of relief that she wasn't on the streets, although they would only be at Shield for one more day.

She ran over to Taylor's bed to wake her up. "Taylor!" she whispered. "Taylor!" she said, a bit louder.

Taylor was still fast asleep.

"TAYLOR!" Morgan said, a lot louder this time. Taylor fell out of the bed and bumped her head.

"Ouch!" Taylor said, massaging her head. Then she remembered. "Oh my God, it's Christmas!"

They both jumped up and down. Then, gradually, Morgan slowed down. "Do you think we're alright to go downstairs?" she asked.

"Don't be daft; no-one's gonna do anything," Taylor reassured her and they went downstairs together.

The tattooed girl and two of the other guys were in the kitchen, having breakfast. The girl scowled at Morgan as she sat down, but she didn't say anything. The two guys talked about sharing a spliff later on.

When they had finished their toast, Taylor and Morgan went upstairs to use the bathroom and get dressed. It felt so good to have a proper shower and Morgan wished she could stay at Shield forever, for a moment. Then she jerked herself back to reality, got out of the shower, got dried off and got dressed.

In the late morning, coming up to twelve, John got some board games out and put them on the table in the living room. The two guys who had had breakfast at the same time as Morgan, Taylor and the other girl had gone out to smoke their spliff together. There was no sign of the other three guys. The other girl kept walking backward and forward between the living room to the kitchen, giving Morgan and Taylor dirty looks.

"What are you looking at?" Taylor said to her.

The girl just muttered something under her breath and then went out of the living room and out of the front door.

"Shall we play a game, Morgan?" Taylor asked.

"Yeah. Not much else to do really, is there?" Morgan replied.

They played Operation, then went on to Scrabble, then they played Blackjack and Rummy. When they had finished their third game of Rummy, the other three guys and the girl came back in. Shortly after that, the two guys who had been smoking their spliff came back in as well. They stank of weed.

"Oh my God," said Morgan. "I hate that smell." It reminded her of a boyfriend her mum used to have who was always smoking that stuff as well.

"Don't worry," John said, and he sprayed some air freshener. Then he turned round and said, "Who wants to play Monopoly?"

Six of them played – the tattooed girl and the guy she'd been kissing on Christmas Eve just sat and talked. They played for a good hour.

It was getting dark outside. John looked at his watch.

"Half past four already?" he exclaimed, a bit startled. "I believe it's time for Christmas dinner."

They all went into the kitchen and John warmed the plates of food one by one and put them out. Everyone tucked in. It was glorious. Turkey, stuffing, ham, roast potatoes, carrots and sprouts all covered in gravy. They drank Shloer and whatever was on the table: brandy, whisky mixed with orange, wine and snowball. Then they had mince pies with cream for pudding.

Afterwards they had another party. The tattooed girl had a bit too much to drink and got rowdy and aggressive. John politely told her to calm down or else leave the room. She wouldn't stop drinking and got even louder and rowdier. Some of the guys laughed. Morgan felt a bit scared but kept dancing and tried not to show it.

The girl's behaviour reminded her of another boyfriend her mum had who had a drink problem. Morgan couldn't understand that sort of behaviour. Over-drinking was never the answer to your worries.

John asked the girl to leave the room. She looked at him then started screaming. A couple of the guys told her to do what John said.

There was no laughing now. There was something seriously wrong with the girl. The two guys had to escort her out of the room because she said she was going to punch John in the face.

After the party, Morgan and Taylor were talking in their room.

"The party was good, wasn't it?" Taylor said.

"I didn't really like it. I didn't like the way that girl was going on."

Taylor looked at Morgan. "I felt a bit sorry for her. When the guys were laughing at her, I mean."

"Why did she get so drunk though? I don't understand why people do it."

"Just for the hell of it, really," Taylor said. "'Cos it's Christmas."

"Mmm. Yeah, I suppose so," Morgan said agreeably. It hadn't been that bad. At least they'd got a decent meal. They would only be there until tomorrow though. Then it would be back to the streets again.

Boxing Day. Back to square one. After that high, they were on a low again. Taylor and Morgan were ready before anyone else. They thanked John for everything and then left.

When they got into town, Taylor fished around in her pocket for some change. She went to Greggs and bought a sandwich while Morgan stood outside, waiting. Morgan didn't have any change to buy a sandwich. When Taylor came out, she asked if she could have some of hers.

"No! It's mine, all right?" Taylor snapped and greedily gobbled the whole thing down.

Morgan was staring. She couldn't believe Taylor wouldn't share with her. On this freezing cold Boxing Day. How heartless could she get?

"Why did you just do that?" Morgan asked her.

"Because I was hungry. Why do you think?" Taylor said to Morgan, talking to her as if she were stupid.

"So am I. I'm starving! What am I going to eat?"

"I don't know," Taylor said. "Get something out of a bin." Then she laughed callously.

"You know something," Morgan said, "I never want to see you again." And she stormed off.

She went back to her usual spot in her usual shop doorway but was surprised to find someone else there. She sighed and stood there for a moment. Then she walked on.

She walked down past the town hall and onto Infirmary Street, then over the little bridge near Woodhouse Square. At the bottom of the bridge, there was a little patch of grass. She decided to stay there. On the evening of Boxing Day, she just slept in her sleeping bag. The day after that, she put up the tent that she had bought a few weeks ago with some money she had saved and stayed there for the next few nights, begging people for change.

She felt so ashamed sometimes. She had never thought it would come to this. She felt like no-one loved her. It wasn't just the weather that was cold – people were cold. The world was cold.

New Year's Eve was finally here. Morgan just wanted this horrible year to end and for things to get better. That didn't look likely at the moment though.

Morgan sat in the doorway of her tent and looked out. Many people passed her by – apart from one lady, a smartly dressed lady with blonde hair. She was thin and wore a red coat with matching red-heeled shoes and a red beret perched on her head. She approached Morgan and bent down. She had a bag in her hand.

"Hello there," she said. "How are you?"

"Fine," Morgan lied. "Never been better."

The lady gave Morgan the bag. "There's a box with a pizza in it in the bag," she said. Then she reached inside her handbag, took ten pounds out of her purse and gave it to Morgan.

"Wow. A whole tenner!" Morgan squealed. "Oh, thank you. Thank you so much."

"It's fine. Take care," the lady said and then she walked back over the bridge and went on her way.

Morgan ate some of the pizza on New Year's Eve and saved some for New Year's Day. It was a New Year – but would things change? Morgan wasn't sure. The hungry feeling in her stomach had gone but the ache in her heart hadn't. Another year had come but the future really didn't look bright for her at the moment. She lay down inside her tent, wondering how she was going to sort her life out.

Chapter 3

The cold month of January had gone quicker than a flash and it was now the beginning of February. This year didn't seem to be looking much better than the last for poor Morgan. The tenner that the kind lady gave her on New Year's Day only lasted a week. Then she had to go back to begging on the streets once again.

She used to feel so small when people passed her and acted like they couldn't see her when she asked for change in the city centre. She didn't even feel like a human being. The whole situation was demoralising, and she really was sick of begging. It wasn't how she wanted to live. So, she started thinking of ways that she could make money.

One day, she was walking through town when she saw someone selling *The Big Issue*. It looked fairly easy and she was sure that you could get money for doing it as well. She approached the man who was selling it to find out how to become a *Big Issue* seller.

He told her everything she needed to know. A couple of days later, she was selling *The Big Issue* as well. Her spot was just outside the train station, so she saw a lot of people. She asked almost everyone she saw going into the station. She said, "*Big Issue*, sir, *Big Issue*, love," until she was tired and her feet were aching from standing on her feet all day.

It wasn't the ideal job, but at least she was doing something. She wasn't just loitering on the streets. She had some money in her pocket as well now. If she kept going, before long she would be able to get temporary accommodation. She had to. She couldn't live on the streets much longer. She was young and vulnerable and needed a roof over her head.

That same night, she went back to spot, put up the tent again and got inside. She ate her little tub of pasta that she had bought. After that, she prayed to God that things would get better and that she would find somewhere to stay.

The cold winter had gone and spring was finally here. Slowly, the leaves were growing back on the trees and the atmosphere was changing. On the 1st March, Morgan counted the money she had made selling *The Big Issue*. She had made enough to stay in temporary accommodation at a place she had heard about, through word of mouth, called Sunnyfield Accommodation.

She took her little tent down and folded it up. Then she put it in her rucksack along with her other belongings and walked over the little bridge near Woodhouse Square and into the city centre to catch the bus, because Sunnyfield was quite a distance away from the city centre. She really hoped that this would be the start of a new chapter in her life.

On the bus, she looked out of the window, keeping her eyes peeled for the Sunnyfield sign. It was on the bus route, she had heard. After ten minutes, she still hadn't seen it. She hadn't spotted it after twenty minutes either.

Suddenly, after twenty-five minutes, she saw a big yellow sign with black writing on it. It said "Sunnyfield Accommodation". She pressed the bell and got up out of her seat. The bus halted as she walked to the front and the doors opened. She thanked the driver and got off the bus.

As she walked through the gate and up the garden path she looked around. It seemed nice enough – there were a few flowers in the grass, and even one or two gnomes. She already felt at home and she wasn't even inside yet.

Knocking on the door, she stood and looked through what she assumed was the living room window. She could see a couple of people sat down chatting. She looked back at the door. At that very moment, the door opened.

A slim lady with a stern face and jet-black hair was standing in the doorway. She looked Morgan up and down.

"Er – hello," Morgan mumbled nervously. "My name's Morgan."

"Hi," the lady said. "Is there something I can help you with?"

"Yes. I've been homeless for a few months and I need somewhere to stay."

"Well, you can't stay here for free, you know," the lady said, as if Morgan were stupid.

"Oh, I know that. I have money and everything."

"Right," the lady said. She didn't seem very friendly. Morgan didn't feel at home any more.

"Please, do you have a room where I could stay?" Morgan asked politely.

The lady was quiet for a moment. Then she said, "I think we have. Why don't you come in?"

Morgan smiled and said thank you. Stepping inside, the warmth of the place filled her body.

"Follow me," said the lady. "My name's Teri, by the way."

"Nice to meet you, Teri," Morgan replied as they walked along the corridor.

They came to an office. Teri asked Morgan to wait outside the door. Then she came back out and asked Morgan to fill in a form. It wasn't that long; it just had the price it was to stay there for one night, for example, then asked you how long you wanted to stay. Morgan wanted to stay until April. After she had filled in the form, she gave it back to Teri, who took her payment.

Then Teri took her to the living room. The same two people Morgan had seen through the window were sitting in there. They both looked up when Teri and Morgan came in.

"This is Dave and Jessica," Teri said to Morgan. And to Dave and Jessica, she said, "This is Morgan, our new girl."

"Hi, Morgan," Dave said, but Jessica didn't say anything.

"Hi," Morgan said shyly.

"Right," Teri said. She looked at Morgan. "Shall we find a room?"

Morgan smiled. She and Teri went up the creaky staircase. They walked down quite a long corridor, which had lots of rooms on either side. Teri stopped outside room thirteen and took some keys out of her pocket. Then she opened the door.

The room was very basic. There was a single bed, which was neatly made, with a small bedside table beside it. There was a wardrobe and a desk with a chair and a large window, which had a view of the garden. Morgan put her rucksack down and said, "Is this where I'm staying then?"

"Well, obviously," Teri said. She gave Morgan a key.

"Thanks," Morgan said. She was slightly concerned about being in room thirteen, because the number thirteen was considered unlucky, but she decided not to say anything to Teri. She didn't seem too friendly. Anyway, at least she had a room now.

After Teri had gone, Morgan flopped down on the bed and stared up at the ceiling. Her head buzzed with thought. She wondered if she would actually make any friends here. She wondered why the girl in the living room hadn't said hi. Girls could be so weird sometimes. The guy seemed okay. Maybe she could make friends with him.

She got up after a while and opened the wardrobe. It had a funny smell and a few wooden hangers inside. She had nothing to put on the hangers though. All of a sudden, she felt really sad. She started crying. She didn't have anything. Of course, she had a bit of money from selling *The Big Issue* but she didn't have enough to buy a whole wardrobe of clothes like she wanted to. And even if she had, who would she go shopping with anyway? She had no-one.

She stayed in her new room for half an hour then got bored and decided to go downstairs. Slowly, she poked her head round the living room door. Dave and Jessica were still there, but they weren't the only ones.

Morgan felt a bit nervous, but she went in. There were two more people in the room apart from her, Dave and Jessica – two young ladies. They didn't talk to her at first and giggled at bit when she sat down on the armchair by the windows. Then one of them said, "Hi, love, are you alright?"

Morgan was relieved about that and smiled and said, "Hi," back. Dave and Jessica seemed to be having their own conversation, so Morgan asked the girls what their names were.

The one who had said, "Hi" to Morgan first was called Natasha. The other one was called Emily. They both had blonde hair, but Emily's was wavier and she was prettier than Natasha. Morgan liked

Natasha more though. Emily seemed a bit standoffish. Morgan had a nice chat with them, but she talked to Natasha a bit more. Emily gave her a funny look, but Morgan wasn't really bothered.

Everyone stayed in the living room chatting for about an hour, then Dave and Jessica left. Morgan waited until they'd left the room. Then, when they had gone, she turned to Natasha and Emily and said, "Don't you think that girl's a bit weird?"

"What do you mean?" Emily said rather abruptly.

"I mean, when I came in a while back, she never even said hi."

"Yeah, she can be like that," said Natasha. "Don't pay any attention to her."

"She's not that bad when you get to know her," Emily admitted. "But I wouldn't bother with her too much."

Then Natasha added, "I actually think she has sex for Dave's money."

The three of them giggled. Morgan looked at Natasha after a bit though and said, "Seriously?"

"Seriously, man," Natasha verified, nodding her head.

"That's probably what she's gone to do now actually!" Emily cackled.

Morgan laughed again but she felt a bit stupid and then said, "I'm going to my room."

"Er, okay," said Natasha, sounding a tad confused.

Morgan got up and the two girls just looked at her and then at each other, but Morgan hardly even noticed. She just went upstairs and sat on her bed.

Her moods changed almost every five minutes over the following week and she felt very scared. She barely spoke to the others. Things became very tense and unpleasant. She knew she would have to go away soon, which would be hard, but she had to do it for herself.

On the second week of her stay, she asked the staff if they could help her look for a flat. They looked at her as if she were berserk at first. Then they said they would see what they could do.

They weren't really that helpful though. It was weeks before they got back to her. And when they did, they wouldn't give her exactly what she wanted. She didn't really care though; she just wanted to get out of Sunnyfield. So, when they said they had found her a room in a youth hostel, she just thought it would make sense to accept it. After all, it was better than nothing.

She was given a place at Open Door Youth Hostel. She was so relieved. She hadn't exactly been getting on with the other people at Sunnyfield's anyway. And at least she would be able to claim benefits now. I'll just have to do better and get on with the people at the youth hostel, she thought to herself.

However, when she got to the youth hostel, she realised that things were going to be even worse. The staff weren't very friendly at all. They gave her a room but they didn't bother taking her up like Teri had done in the accommodation.

It was obvious that she was completely on her own. There were all sorts of people in that hostel and some of them weren't nice at all. They did drugs and made her get involved. She didn't understand why she was doing it even though they weren't treating her quite right. How long was this going to go on for? When was she going to get out of this trap? When would things change? She was finding life so hard, and she felt more lost than ever. But she knew she had to keep going, even though things were getting really hard.

Chapter 4

"Hi, Morgan, how are you?" Morgan's so-called friend Ashley said in a fake voice.

Ashley was only talking to Morgan to be polite, but she hated her. Morgan had a good idea that Ashley wasn't really her friend, but she didn't realise how much she hated her. Or how much some of the other young people at Open Door Youth Hostel hated her. She needed to keep talking to Ashley though, because Ashley wasn't as spiteful as the others.

"Hi, Ashley. I'm all right," Morgan answered, even though she felt terrible.

"Who you answering back?" Ashley said nastily.

"No-one!" Morgan said. "I was only–"

"No-one wants to know, dickhead," someone else said, then they pushed past Morgan in the corridor and went out the front door. Then a group of about four people came down the stairs. One of them asked Morgan what time it was. Morgan didn't even have a watch, but he didn't seem to care.

"Did you hear what I said, bitch?" he said, then he spat in her face and she gasped in shock. "What time is it?"

"I – I don't know. How am I supposed to know?"

"She doesn't even know what time it is," said another one in the group. "She's dumb."

Morgan looked at Ashley as if she were going to help her. But Ashley just smirked and went off with the group. They were always treating her like dirt and making her do drugs and then they just left her on her own. She ran back up to her room and sat on the floor. Hugging her knees, she wondered why she had let herself get into this situation and how she would get out of it.

They told her all sorts of nasty things. She hated the way they did it, and they were always telling her she was ugly. She thought they were lying though, sometimes, and that it was because of her race, but she would never say that. Once or twice, she asked them why they were doing it, but they just laughed in her face and said nasty things about her, right in front of her face sometimes.

Morgan didn't know who to confide in, though. None of the staff cared, so she couldn't tell them. There was a young black man there whom she liked the look of, but she didn't really want to approach him. This was because he spent a lot of time on his own. He hardly even spent time with the other young black people at the hostel. There were four of them and they got on with each other well, but they didn't like him. Morgan didn't understand why. She didn't want to understand. She was so self-absorbed and so trapped that she couldn't even begin to understand what they were doing and what that man was going through. And he wasn't exactly like her, so she just acted like she was better than him and kept company with the others.

Morgan stayed in her room for a good half an hour, sulking because she couldn't cry over the way they treated her. Then she came out and saw two girls, one Indian and one Oriental-looking, coming towards her. They both looked at her and she looked away.

"Wonder what's wrong with her?" one of them said. She didn't even know which one it was but she didn't really care. They had already gone down the stairs. She was just about to start going downstairs when she saw him.

That same guy who always seemed to be on his own. That same guy she was dying to talk to but couldn't even approach. He approached Morgan and smiled at her.

"Hi," he said.

"Er, hi," she said, a bit arrogantly.

"What is your name?" he asked her. He had beautiful eyes. She looked into them for a few seconds, but she never got lost in them.

"Morgan."

"Hi, Morgan. I'm Solomon. How are you doing?"

She didn't even bother lying.

"Not too great," she admitted. Then she started crying.

Solomon looked at her in surprise. He had seen her so many times and thought to himself, I'm not approaching her just yet. Because she thinks she's better than me. He liked her though. He thought she was stunning. He didn't like the way the others were treating her or the way she was crying.

"Are you going to tell me what's wrong?" he asked, then he waited for her to stop crying.

She could hardly stop though. After a while she managed to get some words out. "I don't like what they've been doing to me. You know. Bullying me and leaving me on my own."

"I know how you feel, but you must–"

"One of them," she interrupted, "spat at me this morning. I felt so frightened. I could hardly even talk." Then she started crying even more.

Solomon looked at her. Then he said, "Never mind; he's just doing it because you look different to him. Sometimes I think they are nasty to me because I look different. But you mustn't cry over him, or them, or anyone else."

"What you telling me not to cry for? You don't know what it feels like to be me. You don't even like me. You're probably just talking to me because you feel sorry for me."

"No, no! I do like you. But I think you need to stop crying and talk to me more. Because I'm your friend."

Morgan stopped and looked at him. Then she dried the tears from her eyes. When they got to the living room, she started telling him everything. About how she lived on the streets after her mum threw her out, about temporary accommodation and all the bits in between. He listened intently and said something every now and again, but he was so into her and couldn't take his eyes off her.

"And that is the sad story of my life," Morgan muttered. Then she perked up. "What about you?"

"What about me?"

"Why are you at the youth hostel? Did you fall out with your parents?"

"Well, kind of. I get on better with them now, though. I just don't want to live with them anymore. I don't like it here either. I'm going to get a flat soon because I can't take this shit anymore."

Morgan was quiet. She thought to herself, "What's he talking about? Doesn't he realise what I've been going through?" However, she thought she'd better not ask him this. She just whispered, "Neither can I. I've been taking drugs, but it's only to fit in with them."

"I don't take them at all. It's not funny what you've been doing to yourself, you know. You still look really pretty, but if you don't stop taking drugs, you'll ruin your looks."

"I don't care. I don't even know why you're telling me that." Then she raised her voice and screamed, "I can do what I want! Get away from me, Solomon. I don't even know you."

Solomon gave her a funny look.

"Just remember what I said and that you're really pretty and that–"

"Get away from me!" Morgan yelled but then she started to laugh, and Solomon laughed with her and started telling her how he had been longing to talk to her and that she was stunning and going on and on. She listened and was extremely flattered. She asked him how old he was. He was a couple of years older than her, but he clearly hadn't been through half of what she had been through. At least he was still in touch with both of his parents. At least he got on with them. She couldn't even get on with her parents. She had forgotten all about them and never wanted to see them again.

"Would you like my number?" she asked Solomon.

"Yes! And I'll give you mine."

From then onwards, they were like best friends. They spent almost all their time together. They went for walks in the local park, in town, all over together. Then, they became intimate.

Morgan had never felt this way about anyone before. She had experienced crushes whilst she was growing up, but she hadn't really had a boyfriend before. She'd thought about it, but she never realised she would get this lucky. Solomon never tried to bully her or take advantage of her, even though she was obviously a bit vulnerable.

Solomon was a Christian, so they had their belief in God in common. He helped Morgan to stop taking drugs and supported her. It was like they were in their own little bubble. Morgan hardly spoke to the others any more, and they thought she was acting really weird.

One day, Morgan said to Solomon, "You're like an angel."

She wondered why she had said it at first. Then she started thinking – Maybe he's not as nice as I thought he was. To begin with, everything was so nice. It was like a dream.

They were still intimate, but Solomon didn't want to go out for walks any more, and the spark seemed to have gone already, even though they had only been together for about three months or so. Morgan wondered if he was still into her, or if he just wanted one thing. She didn't dare to ask him though, because she knew it would ruin things.

Morgan was surprised when, at the five-month mark, Solomon asked her if she wanted to get a flat with him. Without hesitation she said, "Yes! I can't wait to get away from this place." Finally, there was a way out for her, a whole new life.

In the late autumn of 2004, Morgan and Solomon prepared to move out of Open Door Youth Hostel. Some of the others looked at Morgan as she came down the steps after Solomon with her bags, but only Ashley asked her where she was going.

"I'm going away," she said, "and I'm never coming back."

"We don't care," one of the others said. Ashley looked completely nonplussed but she smiled and said, "Good luck in life. Bye."

"Yeah," Morgan said carelessly, "bye." And she and Solomon went out the door, down the narrow path and through the gates. Morgan took a little look back and then quickly hurried after Solomon.

They got the bus into town and then another bus over to West Leeds. After they got off the bus, they walked for a further ten minutes until they came to a block of flats. They got the lift and went up to the fourth floor. Solomon gave Morgan a key and opened the door to flat forty-three Carrington Towers with his. After he had gone inside, Morgan took a deep breath and then stepped in, closing the door behind her.

It wasn't what she expected. Then again, nothing ever seemed to be what she expected it to be. The living room was not very spacious, and it still had the last person's wallpaper on its walls. Morgan went into the tiny kitchen and looked around. There were two little cupboards and a place for an oven and a fridge but there was no space for a washing machine. Morgan assumed there was a laundry room on site or else they would just have to use the local launderette.

The bathroom had a bit of mould on the walls. Morgan sighed. Was this really what she had left the hostel for? A pokey little flat in a tower block? It was better than nothing, but still, she felt a bit disappointed.

She went through to the bedroom. It was a bit bigger than the kitchen and bathroom but not as big as she had thought it would be. Solomon came through and hugged her.

"Well," he said as they embraced, "do you like it?"

"Yes," she said, although it was a complete lie. She knew she would just have to get on with life though and be a bit more positive.

That evening they ordered a Chinese takeaway and sat on the floor to eat it. The sun was starting to set now. It was beautiful and Morgan felt so relaxed in Solomon's company. Things weren't perfect, but Morgan had realised that nothing would ever be perfect.

It was one month after they had moved in. Morgan had never been so happy. She couldn't find a job though, which she believed was mostly because of her age. Solomon had a job, and when he got home, Morgan always had something prepared for him to eat. On weekends they would get takeaways and watch a film together, cuddled up on the sofa.

However, Solomon began to notice that Morgan was getting lazier and lazier. She only did a bit of cooking after a while and wasn't really trying to look for a job. He was already getting tired of her and the fact that he had to go out to work and then still do the washing up.

He wouldn't tell her though. He had grown to love her so much that he couldn't even tell her the truth. Morgan loved him as well, but she didn't realise how much he loved himself and that all sorts of things were going on in his head. He was even thinking about leaving her at one point. He had the common sense and understanding to stay with her though, because he knew she didn't really love herself.

Chapter 5

It was the year 2005 now and half of January had gone in the blink of an eye. The weather was icy cold, hardly anyone could be seen on the streets and the atmosphere at Carrington Towers was eerie and quiet. At number forty-three that Saturday, Solomon was making breakfast.

Morgan was still in bed. Then, all of a sudden, she got up, pulled the covers back and jumped out of the bed. She covered her mouth and ran to the bathroom.

"Is everything all right?" Solomon called, but he didn't get an answer. He heard Morgan vomiting.

When she came out of the bathroom she looked awful. She could hardly drag her legs, she was sweating and shaking and she looked very tired. Solomon told her to sit on the sofa and gave her a glass of water. She took her time and drank it, but she was still shaking a bit.

"I don't know why I keep shaking like this, but I feel terrible, Solomon," Morgan said in a voice that was shaking as well. "I'm terrified. What is it?"

Solomon looked at her then looked away. Then he looked back at her with wide eyes. "Morgan," he said slowly, "you don't think you're pregnant or anything, do you?"

"Oh my gosh!" she shrieked. "I never even thought of that."

The very same day, Solomon bought a pregnancy test from Boots. They both went in the bathroom and opened it. Then, Morgan followed the instructions and waited for the result to come up on the screen. When it said "Pregnant", Morgan's mouth fell open in shock. She showed Solomon but he seemed to be lost for words.

"Aren't you pleased?" she said.

There was silence for a long time. Then Solomon said, "Yes. Yes, I'm pleased." He forced a smile and then hugged her. She knew something was up, though.

By then, though, she was so in love with him that she didn't want to see the truth. She just believed they were going to be together forever. He made her happy, so it made no sense to be pessimistic.

When they were having dinner however, he gave her a very weird look. It was a look that said, "I don't want to be with you. I'm just putting up with you." She couldn't understand why he was being so weird all of a sudden, but she knew it made no sense to ask him.

Instead she said, "Why are you looking at me like that?"

"Humph!" he snorted. "Why do you think?"

Morgan felt a bit wounded, but she didn't bother saying anything else. Solomon hardly even looked at her after that. He did the washing up, but he wouldn't talk to her like he usually did.

"Solomon," Morgan said from the living room. "Why won't you talk to me?"

He sighed, finished the dishes and turned to look at her. Then he said softly, "You gonna ring the doctor tomorrow?"

Morgan smiled. She was glad he said something. Maybe he did want to stay with her. Maybe she had been wrong in her thinking.

The next day, Morgan told the doctor she was expecting. They told her to come in two days later, which she did. After she told them she wanted to keep the child, she was given a list of foods she could eat and foods she could not eat, and the doctor had a long discussion with her about pre-natal classes and suchlike.

Morgan was excited at the prospect of having a child, even though she realised she had rushed things. She never wanted to go back to the old life she had, even though she found her new life difficult. Everyone who lived around Solomon and Morgan seemed to be talking about them. Morgan knew some of them were judging her, but she had no time to worry about them or pay any attention to them. She had to think of the baby.

However, about a month later, Morgan got a nasty shock. Solomon asked her to sit down with him one afternoon. She wondered what it was but assumed that he was going to propose to her, which was silly, but she knew it was best.

"Listen," Solomon said. "I'm going to be straight with you."

Morgan looked at him with cautious eyes. Then he said the thing she had always feared he would.

"Now, don't be upset, Morgan, but I don't really want us to be together anymore."

"What?" she said in feigned surprise. "Why?"

"I just don't. I wasn't expecting this to happen." He wasn't telling her the whole truth though. It was really because he thought she was lazy and that she didn't want to do anything with her life. He didn't realise how in love she was though.

She was never going to tell him. But she knew he wasn't being truthful because he wouldn't look her straight in the eye.

"Just tell me the truth, Solomon."

"All right," he said, suddenly raising his voice. "All right. It's because of your laziness. I won't put up with it anymore."

Morgan was gobsmacked. Then all of a sudden, she started begging. "Please, Solomon. Don't leave me all alone. I really need you."

He just looked at her and said with a nasty smile, "But it's you who's going."

Morgan broke down in tears. She looked away from him. Then she got off the sofa and ran into the bedroom. She thought it was totally unfair, but she didn't have it in her to argue or fight with him or even keep begging until she got what she wanted. Because she saw that it was pointless.

So, she packed two bags with all her stuff in, left her key on the table like Solomon asked her to and then went through the door he held open. She looked back at him, tears still in her eyes. He frowned at her then said, "This is your fault, you know," before closing the door in her face.

Morgan spent the night sleeping in a bus shelter. It was freezing cold and she knew she couldn't sleep on the streets again. She knew a bus shelter wasn't the best place to stay either.

So, the next morning, she got the bus and went back to the Open Door Youth Hostel. She felt she had no other option, but as she walked through the gates her palms got sweaty and she trembled. The walk up the garden path seemed to take forever.

Morgan took a deep breath and knocked on the door. A black woman with dreadlocks whom she hadn't seen before stood in the doorway. She looked Morgan up and down.

"And who are you?" she said, her eyes wide open so you could see the whites.

"Morgan Harris."

"Is this the first time you've been here?" she asked, which made Morgan think she was a bit nosey.

Nonetheless, Morgan just admitted that this wasn't the first time she'd been here. She felt a bit depressed about having to admit it though and her shoulders dropped.

"What's the matter?" the woman said bluntly.

"Erm – it's just that I wasn't sure about coming back here. After everything that happened," Morgan told her.

"Mmm," the woman at the door said, nodding. "Well, anyway, my name's Gaynor. I'm the new manager."

"Can I come in then, Gaynor?" Morgan said cheekily.

Gaynor's eyes widened again, but she indicated for Morgan to come in by tilting her head slightly, and then she held the door open for her. She looked at Morgan's belly and then asked her to close the door.

"When are you due, then?" Gaynor asked. She is nosey, Morgan thought to herself. I'll tell her though.

"September; why?"

"No reason." She kept giving Morgan little looks.

Then she asked Morgan to come into her office. They had a brief chat and Gaynor filled in some paperwork and stamped it. And that was that. Morgan was officially back in the Open Door Youth Hostel.

Gaynor gave her a room. It was not the same room she had stayed in before, but it was roomier and more pleasant. There was a little sink near the wardrobe and a landline.

"Well," Gaynor said, "I hope you like it."

"Thank you," Morgan said with a grateful nod.

When Gaynor had gone, she sat on her bed, clutching her stomach. There was a new life inside, an unborn child whom she would have to take full responsibility for. Because Solomon didn't care, and the people at the youth hostel obviously didn't care either.

They were still horrible to her. She figured, though, that if they didn't care about her that it was best not to care about them. There was still a lot of drug abuse in the youth hostel, but of course Morgan stayed out of it this time round. She had to, for the unborn child's sake and for her sake.

She also became more assertive with the youth hostel workers and stood up for herself more. They noticed the difference and put her down on the waiting list for a flat of her own. Within three weeks of her staying at the youth hostel, they had found her a flat and she had moved out.

Morgan's new place was at Berrygate Heights, number three. It was bigger than the flat she had lived in with Solomon at Carrington Towers. This one had two bedrooms, a walk-in shower separate from the bath and an open-plan kitchen. The rent was paid for her by the council because of her circumstances.

On the first night, Morgan slept in the sleeping bag. She had a dream about a man coming on horseback and taking her away, like a prince or something. When she woke up the next morning, she said, "What a silly dream," to herself and had a shower.

It was the end of February now. Although it was still cold, Morgan thought she should go into town and order one or two things from Argos for the flat. The queue went on forever, and when she finally got to the till she was greeted by a pushy sales assistant who was trying to get her to sign up for a loyalty card.

"No, thank you," said Morgan.

"Oh. Okay," the assistant said politely, but she looked angry. Morgan just wasn't interested in these loyalty cards, though. She hardly came to Argos as it was. So, it made no sense signing up for their loyalty card.

Morgan ordered a sofa and a bed. Then she went to Wilkinson's to buy a few things for the kitchen and some toiletries. There were loads of people in town, all going their different ways, some in groups, some with their partners, some alone. Although Morgan felt a bit lonely, she didn't feel so lost any more. And even though her situation wasn't ideal, she knew she would manage, and she could always ask a neighbour if she was struggling.

Week by week, she bought more stuff from second-hand shops for the flat, including a table and chairs and a little wardrobe. Her stomach was slowly getting bigger. She started buying stuff for the baby in April – a pram, a highchair and the equipment to make a cot.

She was a bit confused as how to put the cot together, so she asked her next-door neighbour, Bill, if he could help her. He was reluctant at first, but when she offered him some money, he quickly changed his mind and agreed to do it.

"Right, so, if you'd like to come around at about two o'clock tomorrow," Morgan suggested.

"All right then, Morgan, love," Bill said, nodding.

The next day, he came around and read through the instructions carefully. Then he got his toolbox out and started assembling the cot. He whistled old songs like "Maggie May" as he worked and drank the tea that Morgan made for him. And, in less than an hour, the cot was assembled.

"Wow, that was quick!" Morgan exclaimed. She gave him the money and thanked him for putting the cot together.

"No problem, love," Bill said, and with a smile, he left Morgan's flat. She closed the door and held her bump. Some of the neighbours had noticed it already and one or two had asked her when the child was due. She told them and they said if she needed anything to knock and ask. It felt good to know that people actually wanted to help. She knew she would have to do most of it on her own, though.

She had tried to get back in touch with Solomon several times, but all her calls were rejected. So, eventually she stopped. Sometimes, she cried because she didn't have him, but she didn't worry and was never afraid.

Even though she was more independent now, she wished she had taken her time. She was still so young and hadn't really learnt much about life yet. However, she didn't regret the time she had spent with Solomon and often thought of him and how he had helped her to get off drugs.

He wasn't going to come back into her life any time soon though. It was a bit sad, but she really started wondering when the dream she had had that night would come true. When would her perfect man come and gallantly sweep her off her feet? She had always been romantic but didn't really expect this dream about this man on horseback to materialise any time soon.

Chapter 6

On the 8th September 2005, Morgan gave birth to a beautiful baby girl. She was the tiniest, most delicate thing, with caramel skin and big brown eyes. As soon as she held her baby, she knew it would change her life forever. She named her daughter Abigail.

The nurses observed her bathing the baby a couple of days later. Morgan could feel their eyes on her and felt a bit nervous but gently washed the baby and towelled her dry. Then she put a nappy on the baby and put her in a little baby suit she had brought with her. The baby gurgled and Morgan tickled her tummy. The baby giggled a little. Morgan stuck her finger out and the baby gripped it tightly with her tiny hand, as if she trusted her mother wholeheartedly, as if she never wanted to let go.

Morgan and Abigail stayed in hospital for two weeks altogether and then on the 22nd September, the hospital staff decided it was all right for them to go. A smile of joy spread across Morgan's face, and she got her stuff ready, put Abigail in the baby carrier she had on and then called a taxi. She cooed softly when Abigail started crying to calm her down. The taxi came after ten extremely long minutes. Morgan got in, carefully holding Abigail close to her chest after putting her holdall in the boot.

"Can we go to Berrygate Heights, please?" Morgan asked the taxi driver.

He was a bit unsure as to where it was, but Morgan directed him. They got there within half an hour. She paid him and he said, "All the best, my dear."

"Thank you. Have a nice day," Morgan said, then she climbed ever so carefully out of the car and got the little holdall out of the boot. The car drove off, and Morgan said to baby Abigail, "We're not in the hospital any more, angel."

Of course, the baby couldn't understand fully but she realised things were a bit different now and giggled a little. Morgan felt that a huge weight had lifted and went inside the building.

She unlocked the door to flat number three and switched the light on as she came in.

It felt so strange to be back, although she had only been in the hospital two weeks. She sat the baby on a baby mat she had bought and sat on the sofa. She took a while to relax and looked at her little bundle, realising that this was her child, her responsibility. Abigail looked back up at her with trusting eyes.

Later on, the baby began to cry. Morgan assumed that she wanted milk and breastfed her. A little while later she began to cry again. Morgan got the rattle out and shook it a little to see if that made any difference. The baby calmed down, but yet again, after a while, the crying started all over again.

Maybe she's tired, Morgan thought. Then, she lifted Abigail up and gently put her in the cot. Abigail was still crying. Morgan didn't know what to do at first.

Then, she knew exactly what to do. She sang a well-known song, which was like a lullaby.

"Summertime and the living is easy
Fish are jumping and the cotton is high
Your daddy's rich and your ma is good-looking
So, hush little baby, don't you cry."

Abigail stopped crying. And as Morgan sang the second verse, she fell fast asleep. Morgan gazed at her, the beautiful girl she had given birth to a fortnight ago. She felt lucky to be a mother and was unsure about what was coming next, but she knew she would get by.

The following three months had to be the hardest of Morgan's life. She had so many sleepless nights and everything revolved around Abigail. Morgan had no time to think about herself. Her main concern was making sure the child didn't go hungry and that she was happy.

Sometimes, Morgan thought about asking the neighbours for help because she was struggling. She knew it was best not to though. Everyone had their own problems. And she also wanted to show people she was independent.

One thing she could do now because she had a child was claim Child Benefit. She needed all the financial help she could get really. She wanted to give the child the best start in life, however hard things were. She tried not to look into the future and took it one day at a time, bonding with the child and making the most of what she had.

Morgan had got into the habit of going to the local park with Abigail about three or four times a week. She hated being cooped up in the flat. Abigail seemed to enjoy the fresh air and loved to watch the squirrels run up the bark of the trees and the autumn leaves twirling to the ground.

Although she was getting out of the flat, Morgan still felt a bit lonely. Everyone in her tower block seemed to be in their own worlds; everyone had their worries. She wondered who she could make friends with.

Then she had a brilliant idea.

At the end of January, she joined a creche. She was a bit nervous at first, because she didn't know anyone and they all seemed to have their own friends. As she started talking to people though, she realised they were all in the same boat and they were really similar to her.

She became friendly with two of the other mothers in particular. They were called Amelia and Charlene. Amelia had a little boy called Charlie and Charlene had a little girl called Davinia.

The three of them lived within relatively close proximity of each other. So, Morgan started meeting up with Amelia and Charlene, sometimes in the local park with the babies. They would sit on a bench and talk about their daily lives and how they were coping with everything. These meetings would occur once a week.

One day, in the middle of spring, when they were in the park, Amelia said to the other mothers, "So, where are you guys enrolling your babies? Which nursery, I mean?"

Morgan had not thought about this at all. Charlene said she thought the one near the park was nice and Amelia said she was enrolling Charlie in a private nursery near the city centre. Then both of them looked at Morgan whilst rocking their prams a little.

Morgan paused and then said, "I honestly don't have the first idea."

Charlene laughed, and although it wasn't in a nasty way, Morgan was not too impressed. Which Charlene must have noticed because she stopped laughing and looked at the ground. Amelia just looked a bit uncomfortable, as if she were struggling to find the right words to say.

Then Morgan suddenly exploded. "Well, I'm finding life hard enough as it is without thinking about all that nursery stuff yet! God!"

"All right," Charlene said, "no need to bite our heads off."

Morgan huffed. Amelia looked from Charlene to Morgan then said in a gentle tone to Morgan, "I just brought it up because we'll all have to think about it at some point. I didn't mean to upset you, love."

Amelia and Charlene chatted after that, but Morgan stayed silent. She didn't want to talk; she was angry. After about five more minutes she just got up and started pushing Abigail's pram down the path.

"Morgan?" Amelia said. "Are you all right, there?" Morgan pretended she couldn't hear and carried on pushing the pram until she and Abigail were out of the park.

She was still fuming and people on the road noticed as she made her way home and muttered things like, "What's wrong with her?" She paid them no attention and sighed a breath of relief when she finally got home to Berrygate Heights.

She lowered Abigail gently to the playmat and sat on the sofa. Her phone rang about three times, but she didn't answer it. She just thought about what Amelia had said and how silly she had been. She hadn't even thought about which nursery Abigail would be going to. Maybe it was time to start thinking about it.

Over the next couple of weeks, Morgan looked on her phone for nurseries in the area. She researched about nine different nurseries. She didn't want one that was too far away. Still, she wanted a credible nursery with a good reputation.

Then, she looked at the tenth one. It looked perfect on the outside and nice and spacious on the inside from the photos. There was ivy twisting round the sign where the entrance was. The sign read, "Blueberry Garden Nursery".

Quickly, Morgan wrote down the number. This was the one, she knew it was. She rang them up to find out more about it.

"Hello?" the receptionist said.

"Hello. My name is Morgan Harris, and I just want some information about your nursery. I'm thinking about enrolling my daughter at Blueberry Garden."

"Right, Morgan, what do you want to know?"

First, Morgan asked how old her daughter had to be to start attending the nursery. The lady said fourteen months. Morgan asked how diverse the nursery was. The lady said it was relatively diverse and that parents from a variety of cultures, backgrounds and classes enrolled their children at the nursery. Morgan asked how many members of staff there were and what the name of the nursery manager was. She said there were seven members of staff, including the manager, who was called Anastacia.

"Thank you for telling me more about the nursery. I'll probably ring again when my daughter is a few months older, because it sounds ideal for her," Morgan said.

"No problem," the lady said. "Have a good day."

"Bye," Morgan said.

"Bye now."

In September, when Abigail was exactly a year old, Morgan got her ready and took her to view Blueberry Garden Nursery. Abigail could walk a little bit now. Morgan held her hand and they left Berrygate Heights.

After about ten minutes of walking, Abigail said, "Tired, Mummy," so Morgan picked her up and carried her the rest of the way. It was a sunny day, but the leaves were already changing colour. Before long, they would be falling from the trees again. Morgan could hardly believe her child was already one and that the summer was over.

When they reached the nursery, Morgan pressed the reception button on the wall beside the door and waited. A voice said, "Good morning. Who's there, please?"

"Hi, it's Morgan Harris. I have an appointment to view the nursery."

"Wait a second, Morgan, I'll just check... Yes, you're down for ten thirty a.m. Come in."

There was a buzz and the door unlocked itself. Morgan carefully put Abigail on the floor next to her and pushed the door open. She held the door and whispered to Abigail, "Go inside, sweetheart."

Abigail ran inside the building and held her little hands to her mouth. Morgan came inside and closed the door behind her. She could hear the sound of children laughing, the odd scream, high-pitched little voices talking. Then she looked to the left and saw the receptionist sitting behind a plastic screen. She was on the phone talking to someone. After about a minute, she put the receiver down and pulled the screen back.

"The manager will come out to meet you shortly," she informed Morgan with a smile.

"Thank you," Morgan said quietly. She sat on the soft blue chair and placed Abigail on her lap. She saw the little paintings on the wall that the children had done: flowers, handprints, butterflies. Abigail seemed to like them. She twisted her little head round to look at her mum.

After about five minutes, a petite lady with an oval face, green eyes and mousey brown flyaway hair opened the door to the nursery hall and came into the reception area. She wore a flowery knee-length dress, blue tights and little red boots. She looked at Morgan and smiled, her eyes widening.

"Hello!" she said. "Is it Morgan Harris?"

"Hi, it is, yes," Morgan replied.

"Brilliant," the lady said, then she looked at Abigail. "Hi! What's your name, sweetie?"

Abigail gazed up at the lady.

Suddenly, she was very quiet. Morgan whispered, "Tell the lady your name, sweetheart."

"A-Abigail," she said to the lady, but she wondered who she was. She was excited to be in this place, but it was not the same as other places she'd been to.

"Hi, Abigail, sweetie. My name's Anastacia."

"Stacia," Abigail repeated and clapped her hands.

"Right, Morgan and Abigail, would you like to come with me for a tour of our nursery?"

The three of them went through the door. Anastacia showed Morgan and Abigail the dining area, the indoor play area, where there was a nice Wendy house, the little library, the cloakroom and the outdoor play area. Abigail started jumping up and down when she saw the big sandpit and the children making little sandcastles with buckets and spades.

"Look," one of the children said to the other. "A new girl."

"Hello!" Abigail said, waving.

"Hi," a chubby blond girl said. The rest of them just looked at her. Abigail didn't seem to care though. She was grinning and chuckling and Morgan knew she liked the Blueberry Garden nursery.

Anastacia walked them back to the reception area. "So," she said, smiling tentatively. "What are our thoughts?"

"I think it's the ideal place for Abigail. It has good facilities, and she obviously likes it, so yes," Morgan said, nodding, "I would like to enrol my daughter in your nursery."

"That's fantastic news!" Anastacia exclaimed and she looked really pleased. "They can start at fourteen months."

"I know; she's only twelve months, though," Morgan said. "Mmm. Would it be okay for her to start in January?"

"Of course! Just to let you know though, you must enrol Abigail at least one month before she is due to start. All you need to do is come into the nursery again and then I can do the paperwork with you. Is that okay?"

"Sounds perfect," Morgan said. "Thank you for showing us round today."

"My pleasure," Anastacia said, with a wink. "You press the green button to unlock the door. It was nice to meet to you. Bye!"

"Bye," Morgan said, and Abigail giggled and waved at Anastacia before she went back into the nursery. Then Morgan took Abigail by the hand and pressed the green button to unlock the front door. They went out of the nursery, down the path and began walking home. Abigail didn't get tired this time and managed to walk all the way back to Berrygate Heights with Morgan holding her hand tight.

They had lunch and Morgan played with Abigail. She sang little nursery rhymes to her like "Hey Diddle Diddle" and "Humpty Dumpty". Abigail sat on the mat and sang a little and clapped every now and again. Morgan was happy that Abigail liked the nursery and that she didn't have to worry about it anymore. Only four months until she starts now, Morgan thought to herself.

It was the New Year already. Although the sun was shining, it was the coldest Monday Morgan had ever seen. She had to get ready and get Abigail up though, because it was her first day of nursery.

Morgan felt a bit nervous about leaving Abigail in this place for hours, but Anastacia seemed nice and trustworthy, and Morgan remembered Abigail's face when she visited the nursery – the elation, the joy. She gave Abigail some breakfast but didn't eat anything. She couldn't eat. She had hardly slept the night before for thinking about how today was going to go.

When she had got Abigail dressed, she put her coat on, took some deep breaths and went out of the flat with her daughter. They walked out of the building and didn't stop until they had reached the nursery. Abigail was a stronger walker now.

Morgan looked at Abigail as she pressed the buzzer on the wall outside Blueberry Garden nursery. She looked so cute, in her little pink coat and trousers and afro hair in two little bunches. Then Morgan heard the receptionist's voice.

"Good morning, who's there, please?" the voice said.

"Hello, it's Morgan Harris. My daughter Abigail is starting today."

"Harris... ah yes. Come in, please."

In went Morgan and Abigail; Morgan spoke to the receptionist and she said it was okay for them to go through. Anastacia was not in the main part of the nursery, but a chubby Indian lady approached them with a smile.

"Hello," she said pleasantly. "Are you Morgan?"

"Yes, hi. This is my daughter, Abigail."

"Hi, Abigail!" the lady said. "How are you, pet?"

Abigail looked at the lady and gabbled, "Hello!"

"Sorry, what's your name?" Morgan asked the lady.

"Prishna," the lady told her. "I work here part-time."

"Oh. Well, it's wonderful to meet you, Prishna," Morgan said. "Do you know if Anastacia is in today?"

"She is, but she's a bit busy in her office at the moment."

Then Morgan spotted another lady, thin with glasses and afro hair in twists. She was setting up an activity for the children. She looked up and saw Morgan and Abigail.

"Hi," she said to them. "I'm Esther. Welcome to Blueberry Garden!"

"Thank you," Morgan said, feeling a bit more relaxed now. "I'm Morgan, and this is Abigail, my daughter."

"Oh, hello, Abigail! How are you? Are you excited on your first day?" Esther asked her.

Abigail nodded and squealed. A few minutes later she was playing building blocks with two other children. Morgan talked to the two nursery workers and then Anastacia came into the main nursery area.

"Hi!" she exclaimed enthusiastically when she saw Morgan. "Are you all right! Where's Abigail?"

"She's playing with the other children just over there; she looks really happy," Morgan said. "I'll say bye to her and then I'll pick her up at two thirty p.m. like we arranged."

"No problem," said Anastacia.

"Bye, darling!" Morgan said to Abigail, giving her a little wave.

Abigail waved back quickly and got back to block building. Morgan was reassured by Anastacia that her child would be all right with Prishna and Esther and that was that. Morgan said goodbye to them and went on her way.

When she got home, Morgan could hardly do anything. She could hardly even think for worrying. Would Abigail be all right? Would she get on with the other children? Would she like the food? Because Abigail was a bit fussy when it came to eating.

Then Morgan started wondering why she had even taken her there in the first place. Could these people be trusted? They seemed nice but you never could tell what people were going to do. What if something happened to Abigail? What if she got hurt? It would be all her fault for leaving her at the nursery with those people.

She sat down on the sofa, wondering what to do. She started reading a book but could only concentrate for twenty minutes, then she got all paranoid and worried again. She started hoovering and cleaning. Funnily enough, doing housework always made her feel better.

After that, she thought of what else to do because there were still about three hours left until it was time to pick Abigail up. Then she had an idea. She would make some buns for when Abigail came home.

She got all the ingredients out – the margarine, the sugar, the flour, the eggs and the little chocolate chips. She mixed the margarine and sugar until they were nice and creamy. Then she whisked the eggs and added them to the mixture, then stirred. Then the flour went in, and she mixed before adding some chocolate chips. She mixed them in and pre-heated the oven, then spooned the mixture into the bun cases she had put in the bun tray. She opened the oven and in they went.

A little while later, she smelt a glorious, mouth-watering smell. She took the buns out of the oven. They were a golden-brown colour and looked delicious.

Morgan tasted one. They tasted even more delicious than they looked. Yes, she thought to herself, Abigail will definitely like these.

At about two p.m., Morgan set off to pick Abigail up. She wondered how her daughter had got on as she made her way there. When she finally arrived, the receptionist let her in.

It was only two twenty p.m., so Morgan waited in the reception area for another ten minutes. Then she opened the door to the nursery hall and looked around for Abigail. Esther told her that Abigail was in the Wendy house. Morgan smiled and went over to find her child.

Abigail was sat on the floor inside the Wendy house with a little boy and two other girls. They were clapping and singing a song that Morgan did not recognise. When Morgan poked her head around the corner, Abigail looked round.

"Mummy!" she exclaimed and ran out of the Wendy house to hug her mum.

"How are you, sweetheart?" Morgan asked. "Did you have good day? Are these you friends?"

Abigail nodded enthusiastically and giggled. Then she asked, "Coming back?"

"Oh yes, we're coming back tomorrow. So, you'll be able to see your friends again."

Abigail smiled. One of the girls in the Wendy house said, "See you!" to Abigail. Abigail waved back and then Morgan took her by the hand. She had a little chat with Esther, who said Abigail was very well behaved and that she ate all her dinner. Morgan talked to Abigail, telling her she had a nice surprise for her when she got home. Abigail looked up at her and wondered what it was. A toy? Or a new pair of shoes, perhaps? She didn't know exactly what it was, but she was excited about the surprise.

As soon as they got home, Abigail started running around looking for the surprise. "Slow down!" Morgan said. "You could fall and hurt yourself."

Abigail climbed onto the settee and looked expectantly at her mum, waiting for the surprise. Morgan told Abigail to take her coat off and then went into the kitchen. She reappeared a few moments later with a plate of buns.

Abigail's face up lit up when she saw the buns. She reached her hand out. "Thank you," she said sweetly. She took the little bun out of the wrapper and ate it slowly, looking like she was in heaven.

"So, you like it, then?" Morgan asked.

"Yes, Mummy," Abigail said. She looked at the plate when she had finished, as if she wanted another one.

"All right," Morgan said, "but no more after this one."

"Yay!" said Abigail with delight and took another bun. Morgan laughed to herself and took the buns back in the kitchen. She felt relieved that Abigail's first day of nursery had gone well and that she had made friends. There was nothing to worry about now.

Abigail loved nursery. At weekends, when the nursery was closed, she would sometimes get sad because she couldn't see her friends. When she turned two, Morgan increased the amount of time that Abigail would spend at the nursery.

She didn't just do this because she knew that Abigail liked nursery though. She also did it because she wanted to find a job. She needed a better income and was bored and wanted something to do. Being stuck at home while Abigail was at nursery was driving her crazy and there were only so many times she could look round the shops in town.

So, she started looking for work. She was a bit worried that employers would think she was too young, but she was desperate. At first, the job hunting proved difficult. She had a lot of rejections because of her lack of experience. She applied in all the places she could think of: shops in the city centre, offices and restaurants and cafes but to no avail.

Then, one day she was on the way back home from dropping Abigail off at nursery when she noticed a quirky little cafe on the main road. She assumed it was new because she had never seen it before. She looked through the window. There didn't seem to be anyone in. Maybe they were upstairs. She took a step back and looked up. The sign read "Jose's". Then she noticed a piece of paper in the window. It said:

"Part-time and Full-time
staff needed."

Then it gave a number to ring and whom to speak to if you were interested. Grinning, Morgan looked in her bag for a notepad and pen and wrote down the number and the name – Jose Coutinho. She was tingling with excitement.

It was ideal, because it wasn't too far from where she lived and it wasn't in the city centre, so it probably wouldn't be too busy. Morgan didn't want to work anywhere too busy, actually. Not for her first job anyway.

If she actually got the job, that is. She hadn't even rung them yet. As she walked home though, she knew the job would never be hers if she didn't try. So as soon as she got in, she rang the number.

The phone rang three times, then Morgan heard a man's voice at the other end. He wasn't British; she could tell by his accent. He sounded like he was from Spain or that part of the world.

"Hello, who is speaking, please?" the voice said.

"Hello, my name is Morgan Harris. I'm ringing about the advert I saw in your cafe window."

"Oh yes, of course." There was a short pause and Morgan heard the sound of papers ruffling.

"Have you worked before, Morgan?"

"Er, no, I haven't," Morgan confessed, her voice a little tentative.

"Do you have any catering qualifications?"

"No."

"Mmm. We do prefer it if you have experience."

"Sorry, is it Jose?"

"Yes, it is."

"Well, the thing is, Jose, I really need this job. I've applied for loads of other jobs, and I don't seem to be getting very far. I'm very focused and hard-working and I learn new skills quickly. Please give me a chance."

"You sound like you've had a hard time recently, Morgan," Jose said.

"It has been hard."

There was another pause. "Okay, how about you drop by for an interview on Thursday at one p.m.?"

This was perfect for Morgan because Abigail world be at nursery. "Yes! Yes, I'll be there."

"All right. See you Thursday, Morgan. Bye."

"Bye!" Morgan squealed with excitement. She put the phone down and wrote the interview in her diary.

It was Wednesday night. Morgan had been into town while Abigail was at nursery to buy some smart clothes for her first ever interview. She bought a white shirt and a light-blue blazer and skirt along with some stilettos. She hung them in her wardrobe door and flopped into her bed.

Abigail had fallen asleep about an hour ago. All Morgan could hear was the sound of her own thoughts. What would Jose look like? Would he be nice? He sounded nice enough on the phone, but you could never tell for sure unless you met people in person. What sort of questions would he ask? Would she be able to answer them? She had looked up possible interview questions on the internet to give her an idea, but she didn't really know what to expect, because he could ask her anything.

She knew one thing though. She had to get this job. She couldn't take any more rejections. It was really getting her down. So was hardly having anything to do. She needed something to get up for.

As she got into bed, she tried to think positive thoughts. She told herself the interview would go well. She told herself she had it in the bag. She was young and full of life and ambition, which she knew would come across – nothing could stand in her way.

Chapter 7

The day had finally come. Morgan woke at the usual time, around six thirty a.m. She got into her interview clothes and looked in the mirror after she did her makeup. A nervous Morgan looked back at her.

She got Abigail ready for nursery – Abigail started at nine thirty a.m. Morgan made jam on toast for Abigail's breakfast. She took ages to eat it for some strange reason and kept looking at her mum, wondering what the smart clothes were for. She was used to seeing her in jumpers and jeans.

Because of Abigail taking so long to eat breakfast they left later than usual. And she dawdled a lot as she held her mother's hand on the way to nursery. After a few minutes, Morgan got quite impatient. "We're going to be late if you don't hurry up," she snapped.

Abigail suddenly burst into tears. She wasn't used to Morgan being like this. What was making her act so differently?

"Oh Abigail, just cut it out," Morgan said, but Abigail wouldn't. Morgan felt a bit guilty about being impatient with her child, but it was mostly because she felt so nervous about the interview. Abigail was melodramatic by now and wouldn't walk, so Morgan picked her up and carried her the rest of the way.

As soon as they got through the nursery door, Abigail stopped crying. Prishna was there. "Oh hello! We thought you weren't coming today."

"Sorry we're late. Abigail – er – well, she's a bit upset."

"What's wrong, my dear?" Prishna asked Abigail, who sniffed and looked at her.

"I'm not sure what it is, Prishna," Morgan said when Abigail wouldn't respond.

"Where do you want to play today?" Prishna asked Abigail with a smile.

"Sandpit! Sandpit! Sandpit!" Abigail squealed and she jumped out of Morgan's arms to the ground.

"Well, look at that – she's better already!" Prishna said, laughing. "You look smart, Morgan."

"Thank you, I've got an interview later."

"That's brilliant. I hope you get the job."

"Yeah. I hope so too. I'm a bit nervous though. It's the first interview I've ever had," Morgan admitted.

"They're always the hardest," Prishna said. "Once you've got the first one out of the way, they become easier. I'm sure you'll get the job though. Just think positive."

"I will. Well, I'd better get going. I'll see you at three thirty p.m. Bye."

"Bye," Prishna said. "And good luck."

Morgan nodded appreciatively and then made her way out of the door. She went into town to do some shopping. When she got back home, it was 12.05 p.m. The interview was in less than an hour.

She didn't bother to unpack. At first, she wondered if she should call a taxi, but she wasn't sure how prompt they would be. So, she walked to the cafe instead.

It took her over half an hour to get there and her feet were killing her when she reached her destination. Maybe stilettos hadn't been the best choice of footwear. She was gasping for breath. She took a swig from her water bottle and then looked at her watch. It was quarter to one.

Fifteen minutes until her interview! Eeek! The cafe door was open, so in she went. She looked to the left and saw a few empty tables. Then she looked to the right and saw a man with jet-black hair and slightly tanned skin sitting at one of the tables. He was looking down at his notepad. Morgan cleared her throat to get his attention.

He looked up. "Oh hello, you must be Morgan," he said and he stood up.

"Hello," Morgan replied. "Yes, I'm Morgan." Her heart was in her mouth.

"We can start early if you like, Morgan," the man said.

"Oh. Yes. Yes, okay, let's start early," Morgan agreed.

"Come and take a seat," he said, beckoning her to come over.

Very tentatively, Morgan walked to the table. As she got closer, she felt more and more scared. She sat down on the chair, placing her bag carefully on the floor.

"First of all, my name is Jose, and I am the manager of this cafe. I am looking for five workers to help me run the business. I have already interviewed twelve people and have six more to interview, including you, Morgan. Please tell me why I should employ you."

Morgan took a deep breath.

"Well, I'm hard-working, I have a lot to bring to the table–"

"Like what?" Jose asked.

Morgan paused to think for a second.

"I will always make the effort with people and give one hundred and ten percent. I think I'm a people person and that I get on with others easily. I have a lot of ambition and if you give me this opportunity, I will take responsibility for my own development."

Jose looked up at her every now and again to ask her questions and then took notes as she answered them. Morgan watched him. He had big brown eyes and was handsome. He smelt nice and was well dressed. She liked what she saw.

"And lastly, what skills do you hope to gain at Jose's?"

"I want to work on my communication skills, because although I'm confident, I'm not always good at getting my point across."

"That's definitely something we can work on, so don't worry. But it is important that you co-operate. I hope you mean everything you say about taking responsibility. But, you know, we will see. Right, Morgan do you have any questions for me?"

"Yes. Do we have to wear a uniform?" Morgan asked.

"You can wear what you like, but you must wear the Jose's apron over your clothes."

"All right, that's cool. That's it; I don't have any more questions."

"Then you may go. Thank you for a wonderful interview, and I will let you know by next Tuesday if you are successful in getting a job here at Jose's."

Jose reached out a hand and Morgan firmly shook it. Then they said goodbye to each other. Morgan picked up her bag, got up and left the cafe.

The interview had only lasted twenty-five minutes, so it was nowhere near time to pick Abigail up. Morgan went home and unpacked the shopping. She wondered if she had got the job. She thought the interview had gone well enough. Well, that is to say, for her first one. She got changed into her jeans and shirt.

On her way to pick up Abigail, Morgan bought a little cupcake from the bakery. When she got to the nursery, Abigail and all the other children were doing the 'Hokey Cokey'. Morgan spotted Abigail. She looked so much happier than this morning. Morgan smiled and waited until they had finished.

One of the other children said to Abigail, "Your mum's here." Abigail turned around and the moment she saw Morgan, she ran to her and they hugged.

As they walked home, Morgan explained to the child that she hadn't meant to upset her this morning. "It's was a big day for mummy today," Morgan elaborated. "It was mummy's first job interview."

Abigail wondered what an interview was. She knew it was important because her mum had been acting so differently that morning. When Morgan revealed that she had a special treat for her however, she jumped and giggled and said, "Oh, thank you, Mummy!" So, all was well again.

Things got even better when Monday came. Morgan was getting Abigail ready for nursery when the phone rang. Morgan ran to the phone and picked it up in excitement. It had to be Jose.

"Hello?" she said.

"Hello, Morgan. This is Jose. How are you today?"

"I'm good."

"Well, you'll be even better soon. Because I'm offering you a job."

Morgan's jaw dropped. "Oh, my. Oh, my goodness!" she said. She was all giddy and nearly dropped the phone.

"Do you accept my offer?" Jose asked.

"Yes! Absolutely. Oh, thank you! I can't tell you how grateful I am. Thank you a million times."

"So, Morgan, you will be on probation for two weeks and–"

"Probation?" Morgan said, shocked. "What's that?"

"I need to see if you're right for the role. So, you need to give everything in those two weeks. Or it will be goodbye, and you will sadly have to go somewhere else."

Morgan hadn't expected this, but she was determined to show him what she could do. "When does probation start?" she asked.

"Friday, at nine forty-five a.m."

Abigail usually started nursery at half past nine. Morgan had to make this work though, so she said to Jose that she would be there on Friday. Then, when she got to the nursery, she spoke with Anastacia about bringing Abigail in at nine a.m. so she would have more time to get to work. Anastacia said it was fine and congratulated Morgan.

When Morgan got home, she did the washing and hoovered the floor. Then she plonked herself on the sofa and tried to get her head round the fact that she had been offered her very first job.

Wow! The excitement. There would be all sorts in store for her, she was sure of that. Would she live up to expectations? She had to. She must do what Jose said and give it everything she had.

Morgan would start at nine forty five a.m. and finish at two p.m., which gave her enough time to drop Abigail off at nursery at nine a.m. and pick her up at two thirty p.m., because the cafe wasn't that far from the nursery. There would be six other people on probation, so seven altogether, and there were five jobs available. Morgan had to give herself a good chance and make sure she got on with everyone. She wanted it to look good and show that she was easy to work with and that she deserved the job. She couldn't let this opportunity slip through her fingers.

Morgan thought her first day at Jose's would be a disaster. She dropped Abigail off at the nursery five minutes late, which meant she was a bit behind schedule. After she left the nursery, she went as quickly as she could up to the cafe. She kept checking her watch, hoping she wouldn't be late. She started running in a panic. She had to make it on time.

And she did. Even though she was completely out of breath. It was 9.41 a.m. when she reached Jose's. Everyone else was there already – there were three other female candidates and three male candidates. When she came in all out of breath, hair all over the place, sweaty and disgusting, they all just looked at her then looked at each other.

Morgan herself didn't know where to look. Then she saw Jose. He looked her up and down with one eyebrow raised.

"Hello," Morgan said, breathing hard.

"Hello, Morgan," Jose said. "I'll give you a second to catch your breath..."

"Er, thank you," Morgan mumbled.

Jose walked over to Morgan.

He pointed to a door at the back of the shop. "Go through and leave your bag and coat in there, please," he said sternly.

Morgan walked briskly to the door while the others watched her. She could feel her cheeks going red. She didn't really like the way they were looking at her.

When she came back out, they did it again. She tried not to let it bother her. After all, they were just like her, weren't they?

Jose cleared his throat loudly. "All right. Now that we are all here, we can start what is going to be a very long day for you guys."

He went on for what seemed like an eternity about all the rules and regulations, what to do in case of a fire or any other emergency, what he expected of them and that kind of thing. Then he reminded them that there were only five jobs, so they really had to give it all they had. Morgan took a deep breath and nodded.

"Right. Now," Jose announced, his eyes widening, "time to – how do you British say it? Break the ice?"

There were one or two groans. Morgan didn't groan but she felt her stomach tie itself in knots. She hated ice-breaking. She remembered when she had had to do it when she first started high school and how scared she had been.

It wasn't that bad, though. All they had to do was tell everyone their names and one interesting fact about each other. Morgan told them about her daughter. They all gasped in surprise and one of them turned to the person on the other side of them and said, "But she looks so young!" Morgan smiled shyly and looked at her feet then quickly looked back up when she realised Jose was watching her.

"Okay, guys," he said, although he was still watching Morgan, "let's get this show on the road!"

They had to do several exercises in the first half of the day. They were in two groups: one had three, the other four. Jose also gave them scenarios, and they had to put their hands up and give an answer to the scenarios. Morgan couldn't have been more enthusiastic – she answered three out of the ten scenarios Jose gave them. She wasn't going to let someone else get the job she wanted. It had her name on it.

At twelve p.m., they had a half-an-hour lunch break. Jose said it was up to them what they did. Three of them went out to buy food, but Morgan and the others had brought food with them. They spoke amongst themselves, and half an hour disappeared just like that.

The second half of the day consisted of each of them learning how to use the coffee machine. Jose showed them how to make the perfect cappuccino and then they all had to follow suit. They looked nervously at each other when he said, "Who is going first?"

Then Morgan said, "I will."

Jose motioned towards the machine and Morgan went for it. She spoke out loud, saying which bit she had to do next to the group – it made it easier for her to say it out loud. She sprinkled the cappuccino with chocolate just like Jose had done. When she had finished, Jose tasted it.

"Very nice!" he said. "Although I think it could be a bit creamier. But good for your first try, Morgan. Who is next?"

They all had their turn and Jose sampled each one. Then, they did a couple more tasks and after that it was time for paperwork.

Morgan was so glad when the clock said one fifty five p.m. and Jose said there were only five minutes left. At precisely 1.59 p.m., Jose said they could get their things and go. There was a mad rush to the door out at the back of the shop. Morgan was the last one to go through the door.

"How did you find it?" one of the girls said to her. Her name was Anna, and she and Morgan had spoken at lunchtime.

"It was better than I expected," Morgan admitted.

"I thought it was so hard," Anna said. "Especially cappuccino making."

"It'll probably get easier next week," Morgan reassured her.

"We hope," Anna said with her fingers crossed.

They all piled back out onto the cafe floor. "See you guys at the same time on Monday," Jose said with a smile. His teeth were perfectly straight and gleaming white. He was ridiculously perfect.

Everyone said bye and left the shop. Morgan walked to the nursery and was five minutes early for Abigail, the opposite of that morning when she had dropped her off five minutes late. She walked her daughter home, talking to her along the way, listening to the child telling her little things about her day, about how she and Penny had played dolls and how Drake had fallen into the sandpit.

Morgan felt that her first day had gone quite well – she had done her best anyway. She couldn't wait until next week. She was really going to show Jose what she was made of so he would have no choice but to give her a job.

As soon as they got home, Morgan sighed a huge sigh of relief and Abigail asked her what was for dinner. When Morgan announced it was fish fingers and mashed potato, Abigail squealed, because it was her favourite. It had been a long day and although it had been fun, Morgan was overjoyed to be home, because she hadn't always had a home.

The next two weeks went quicker than a flash. On the last day of probation, Jose got them all together. This must be it, Morgan thought. He must be announcing who gets a job and who doesn't.

"First of all, I just want to say that you have all worked hard over the past two weeks and that you will all have a good future, whatever happens," Jose said. "As you know, there are five jobs, so two of you will be leaving us."

Morgan's heart was beating so loud she was sure everyone could hear it. She crossed her fingers behind her back. Please, she thought to herself, I want this so badly. Of course, she couldn't say anything though.

"I have made my decision," Jose announced. "The people who will be staying here at Jose's are Anna, Marnie, Phoenix, Ashley and..."

Morgan closed her eyes. Please say Morgan, she thought. Please.

"... Morgan."

Morgan opened her eyes and her mouth fell open. She had got a job!

"Jessie and Dane, I'm sorry but it's the end of road for you. Good luck in your careers," Jose reassured them.

Jessie looked at the floor a bit sadly but said, "Thank you, bye," and then left.

Dane asked, "Why didn't I get through?"

"I just don't think you're made for this sort of work, that's all, Dane."

"Oh. Fair enough. I'll be going then. Bye bye." He smiled and then walked out of the cafe.

Jose turned to the rest of them. "Well done, guys!" They all grinned at each other. Jose gave them their aprons.

"Now you are officially working for me," Jose declared. "I'll see you all at the same time on Monday. Have a happy weekend."

They all said bye to each other and then the five new workers left. Morgan went to pick Abigail up. She felt so light, like she was walking on air. Finally, she had got what she wanted, and she never had to look back.

Morgan and the others came to the cafe on Monday morning. Jose looked from one to the other and then paced up and down.

"Right, this is going to be very difficult, but you've all got to work really hard, because in my cafe, no-one goes home early before they've done all their work. I really don't want to be mean to you all," he said, a bit sarcastically, "but if you think you can clean tables all day long, you are wrong. You are not really doing the same thing all the time either. And don't think you're going to get away with not doing anything, Morgan."

Morgan looked at him and frowned a bit, but she didn't say anything. She wasn't really surprised but she looked shocked. Why's he talking to me like that, she thought.

He went on and on and then made them all do different jobs. Every now and again he told them to swap. He shouted at them and ordered them around and swore at them. Particularly Morgan. He wasn't very nice to her at all.

The bullying continued for weeks. Jose always seemed to make Morgan do more work than the others. She really felt singled out and like she was being isolated by the other workers as well. When she was being told off, they just looked at her and did not even bother to say anything to defend her. Morgan would do what Jose said but she knew the way she was being treated wasn't quite right.

Then one day she decided that she'd had enough. After dropping Abigail off at the nursery, she walked up the road determinedly until she got to the cafe. She went up to Jose and asked him if they could talk about something.

"About what, Morgan?" he replied, smiling, as if he didn't know what she was talking about.

There were a few people in the cafe and two other workers, but Morgan didn't care. "Listen," she said firmly. "I don't like the way you've been speaking to me. It's not right. It's not fair, the way I've been picked on and how you're always making me do more work than the others. You always think you're right as well, but you're not. I think you're a bully."

"I don't care what you think," Jose said. "I'm the boss and you do what I say. Who do you think you are?"

"I don't really need to do everything you say," Morgan said, raising her voice, "and you are a bully. I'm not taking your shit anymore."

Jose's mouth fell open in shock. Then his expression became a bit sterner, and he told her something she didn't expect. "I like how you just stood up to me, but I do not like your attitude. What about the way you've spoken to me? You're very impolite, and you need to know yourself better and realise that I have more experience in the world than you. Listen to me when I say that you'll get nowhere in life with that attitude."

Morgan stayed quiet for a bit then said, "Okay, okay, I'll listen more, but you have been bullying and–"

"Just shut up and get on with your work," Jose snapped.

Morgan huffed and went behind the counter. Phoenix and Marnie were working and talking to each other. She said to them, "I don't like the way he treats me. But the way you two and the others have been acting is a bit weird."

"How do you mean?" Marnie said.

"Leaving me out and hardly talking to me."

"Serves you right," said Phoenix. "And really, who do you think you are? Jose is the boss, and you're so rude. It's not your cafe, you know."

Marnie sniggered and then said, "Oh, don't be nasty to her." She didn't sound like she meant it though. Morgan turned away from them and then went to put her stuff in the back. She didn't think her first job would be like this. She thought they'd get on really well. She just didn't understand why Jose was giving her such a hard time, but she couldn't really go back to living on benefits. It was a real struggle she had but that was behind her. She loved her job, and she was never going to leave to please them or give them what they wanted. She had a fight on her hands, and she was going to win.

Walking to work one day, Morgan noticed a man on the street. He was sat on the ground; his clothes were scruffy and dirty and there was a hole in his shoe. He had his little brown cap on the floor and he was looking down at it. There was only a bit of silver and some coppers in the cap and he looked as miserable as sin.

Morgan felt a bit sorry for him and put three pounds in. Then she thought about walking away, but she said to him, "Don't you think you should go to the shop and by a sandwich or something? You've really got to stand up for yourself as well. Else this will just keep happening to you."

The man just looked up at her and said, "Have a blessed day, love."

Morgan smiled and then walked off. She was thinking about how she was going to get through the day. Each day seemed to get harder than the one before. It was like she was climbing a mountain that she was never going to reach the top of. It was exhausting her. She had to survive and keep the job though. She knew Jose hated her, but she didn't really care anymore.

Jose came up to Morgan and then said to her, "Good morning. How are you?" He actually sounded like he cared as well. For once.

"Hello. I'm... okay," Morgan answered.

"You don't sound okay."

"I saw a scruffy man on the street this morning. He looked so down and out. I gave him some money because I felt a bit sorry for him."

"Well, that's nice," Jose said. "How do you know he isn't trying to feed a drug habit or something, though? I don't give them money. And I know I have rights in this country. I work hard, so why give my money to anyone?"

Morgan couldn't believe Jose's stinginess. She knew he was right, but she didn't understand why he had to be right all the time. He really didn't seem to understand her and what she'd been through either. She didn't want to tell him about the fact that she felt sorry for homeless people because she was homeless once.

Maybe she was being too secretive. Maybe she should let Jose know. Morgan just watched him prancing around in his designer clothes and thought, "I wonder who he thinks he is." She didn't really have the nerve to say it to him though. Definitely not to his face, anyway.

Morgan was grateful to have a job. And although things weren't ideal, she thought back to the time when she had no money in her pocket. It was such a struggle she'd been through to get to where she was. How could she throw it away? No, it was her workplace as well. Life was much better, and she had to think of her child as well as herself. She was going to stay there for as long as possible and hang on in there.

Chapter 8

It seemed like just yesterday that Abigail had started nursery, but now she would be starting primary school. Morgan had found her a place at Redmill Primary School. Abigail was very scared on her first day and kept asking her mum if she would see her friends from nursery again.

"No, Abigail. They're going to different schools and you'll just have to make new friends. But don't let them walk all over you. Because some of them think they can. Stand up for yourself and be proud of who you are."

Abigail looked at the ground, but she smiled and nodded, then looked up and said, "Yes, Mummy."

They got on the bus and Abigail sat by the window. She held her mum's hand tightly and kept asking her questions like, "What will it be like? Will they be like me? What do I do if they don't want to be my friend?"

"Just do what I said," Morgan reassured her. "You'll be fine. And remember to smile as well and talk to the other children. Then you will make friends."

When they arrived at the school, Abigail started crying and saying she didn't want to go in. Morgan crouched down and said, "It's only going to be a little while before I collect you. Just be really strong for me."

Then, Morgan and Abigail came through the door and waited in the corridor. They weren't the first to arrive, because Morgan could hear the children chattering and playing and then she heard a woman's voice say, "I'm just going to see who this is out in the corridor."

A woman with short hair and very old-fashioned clothes appeared in the doorway. She was fat and looked a bit wrinkled and old, but she smiled and said, "Hello! Welcome to Redmill Primary School. And who do we have here?"

Abigail wasn't aware that she was being spoken to. Morgan sighed then said, "Tell the lady your name, darling."

Abigail shook her head and tried to back out, but Morgan blocked the entrance and gave Abigail a hard look. "Listen, you're going in. Whether you like it or not. Now, tell her your name."

There was a long silence. The teacher said, "All right, sweetie, I'll tell you my name first. I'm called Mrs Mayor. There's no need to be afraid."

Abigail smiled but still wouldn't tell her first teacher her name.

"Her name's Abigail," Morgan said.

Mrs Mayor reassured her. "Everyone's scared today. We can't stay out here forever, though, sweetie."

Abigail took one last look at her mum and then said, "Well, can I come in then, Mrs Mayor?"

"I'll go now," Morgan said. "Take care of her."

"Don't worry, I will," Mrs Mayor said.

Then Morgan picked up her bag and went through the playground and out of the gate. She couldn't help worrying a bit, because although Mrs Mayor seemed pleasant, she looked a bit insane. She was assertive enough but obviously didn't know what she was doing. What if Abigail didn't stand up for herself and Mrs Mayor couldn't really do much to help her? She had the whole class to oversee.

There wasn't much point worrying about all this now, though. Work started at ten fifteen a.m. today. While she was on the bus, a feeling of dread started to fill Morgan's body. She was really not enjoying work at the moment. She hated having to work with the other people. It felt like they were against her and that there was no way she could escape from the situation or make it any better.

Morgan had only been late once or twice but Jose would exaggerate and say, "You're always late, every morning. Why can't you turn up on time? I'm sick of your attitude!"

Sometimes, Morgan thought it was because of the way she looked. Because she was not exactly from the same place as him.

She knew it would be foolish to say this though. And how did she know it wasn't for another reason? Maybe he just liked picking on her because she was more sensitive than she looked. She hated the way he singled her out, though. She felt like a complete victim.

Who could she tell, though? She couldn't really complain to the boss because he was the boss. And the other workers didn't really see things from her point of view. So, there was no use moaning to them about him.

Morgan got off the bus and started walking to the cafe. She didn't really feel like today was going to be a good day. She just had a feeling. She walked as slowly as possible because she was a bit scared about going in. Then after a while, she looked at her watch. It was twenty past ten.

She panicked and started running. Within ten minutes she was there. As soon as she had stepped over the threshold, Jose saw her and the furious expression on his face terrified her. She waited for him to speak first, but she said to herself, he's not belittling me this time.

"If you're late one more time," Jose seethed, "that's it; you're fired."

"It's not really up to you whether I stay here or not, is it?" Morgan said cheekily.

"What? You don't come in here late and–"

"Listen, I do my work. I do everything that's asked of me. I never moan or complain. Not once have I disobeyed you. And you think it's funny to hold things against me? And to victimise me like this? Well, I'm letting you know something. You do not underestimate me and what I can do. I'll take you to court if you don't leave me alone. Because this is harassment."

For once, Jose was speechless. He stood in front of Morgan with a shocked expression on his face. People in the cafe were looking at him and Morgan. Some of them sniggered and one said, "Who does she think she is?" Morgan was serious though. "You don't care, do you? All you care about is yourself and how big your bank balance is."

Then Jose hit the roof. "How dare you assume that! What about you? Count yourself lucky you even have this job! Your attitude is terrible!"

Morgan bent her head and looked down at her feet. She felt so small and embarrassed. Maybe she should have kept her mouth shut, but it was too late now.

"Get out of my sight and clean those tables," Jose ordered.

Defeated, Morgan started wiping the empty tables down. She was almost in tears. Why did he always have to win every argument? Why was she always in the wrong? She just couldn't work it out.

After work, Morgan picked Abigail up from school. Abigail was very chatty and talkative, telling her mum about what she had done, about how they had been learning about the seasons and painting, and Mrs Mayor had read *The Very Hungry Caterpillar* to them before home time.

Morgan only half-listened. She was still in a mood because of what had happened at work. Abigail picked up on this and said, "Are you listening, Mummy? Are you alright?"

"Hmmm? Oh, yes, Mummy's fine. What do you want for dinner tonight?"

"You weren't listening, Mummy. Something's wrong, isn't it?"

"Don't be silly, Abigail," Morgan said. "Nothing's wrong."

When they got home, however, Morgan was so miserable she could hardly cook the dinner. They just ended up having a takeaway pizza. She couldn't concentrate or focus enough to make a proper meal.

Abigail ate about two slices and then said, "I can't eat any more, Mummy."

"It's all right. I'll put the rest in the fridge, sweetie," Morgan responded.

A couple of hours later, she tucked Abigail in and then closed the door behind her. She tried to escape by reading a book, but she felt too upset and hopeless to even do that. She threw the book to one side and then got ready for bed.

Morgan tossed and turned but she couldn't get to sleep. She thought of work that day and started crying. She hit the pillow in anguish. What a horrible man I have for a boss, she thought. Why is he so mean to me?

She really couldn't stop thinking about him. She wanted to hate him, but she couldn't. Although she didn't like the way he treated her, she was starting to crush on him. Which made things even more uncomfortable.

Maybe things would change. Maybe she just needed to change her attitude and stop believing she was a victim all the time. Maybe that would make things better.

Chapter 9

At Jose's, things were still a bit tense. It was now late September, and although the argument between Morgan and Jose had been a couple of weeks ago, that day was still very stuck in Morgan's head. She couldn't erase it.

How could she win him over? She knew he was stubborn and bad-tempered, but it couldn't be impossible to change his opinion of her. She had to, so they could work with each other.

Morgan became more humorous and smiled more. And when Jose said something negative or critical, she wouldn't take it to heart. She was starting to develop a thicker skin without being difficult or unfriendly. She thought Jose still had it in for her but just wanted to get on with him better, because she didn't really want to lose the job. She liked working at Jose's.

Jose noticed the effort Morgan was making. He really began to warm to her and started talking to her more, about all sorts of things they had never spoken about before: hobbies, places they liked to go, likes and dislikes and all that jazz. Within a very short period of time, they because a lot closer.

One Friday night in early December, before Morgan was about to get her things with the other workers, Jose said, "Morgan, can I ask you something?"

"Come and sit down at the table," Jose said. "I need to talk to you." His tone was serious.

Morgan thought to herself – Oh no, am I in trouble? Yet again?

After the others had left, Jose looked at her. Then he said, "We have known each other for a long time. I didn't like the attitude you had at first. Especially because I gave you an opportunity and you didn't seem grateful."

Morgan listened.

"Recently, though, I feel like things are changing between us. In a good way, of course."

"So … what are you saying?" Morgan asked, not sure where the conversation was leading.

"Would you like to go out on a date, Morgan?" Jose asked, and he smiled his perfect, flawless smile.

Morgan sat there, gawping at him. It didn't register at first; it was almost like it wasn't really happening. Jose couldn't really be asking her out on a date.

After a few moments, though, she processed the question and gave the polite answer, "I'd love to."

"Good. I was thinking of that new restaurant, in the city centre, called Olivio's," Jose said.

"Sounds good to me," Morgan agreed.

"I will book the table for eight p.m. tomorrow night," Jose said. His voice was stern again, all of a sudden.

Morgan straightened up. "All right," she said softly. "See you tomorrow night."

"Goodnight," Jose said.

Morgan got up and left the cafe. As she walked along, her whole body was filled with a warm, beautiful feeling she had never felt before. A date with Jose! She never could have predicted this. As she smiled and made her way home, she felt like the luckiest girl in the world.

On Saturday morning, the first thing Morgan did was phone her neighbour, Rosie, to ask her if she could babysit for her that night. Morgan had got to know Rosie well. She was a considerate lady and had given Morgan one or two lifts and helped her with shopping. Morgan offered her forty pounds to babysit and everything was arranged.

After she and Abigail had had breakfast, Morgan told Abigail to get washed and dressed and do some colouring in. Then, whilst Abigail was in the bathroom, Morgan began to look through her wardrobe. She needed to find the perfect outfit for the date with Jose.

It took her almost three hours to choose one. She "ummed" and "aahed" at all her dresses and thought to herself, "That one's too over the top; my bum looks big in that one; that one's not in any more." Then she noticed one she had bought quite recently. A beautiful emerald-coloured dress. It was a fitted dress and was off the shoulder and sexy. That's the one, Morgan thought. He won't know what's hit him when he sees me in this number.

At about six p.m., Morgan got dressed in the emerald number and put on her six-inch heels. She wore shimmery gold earrings and green eyeshadow with a little bit of blusher and peach lip gloss. Abigail looked at her when she came out of her room.

"Why are you wearing that dress, Mummy?" Abigail asked, wondering where she was going.

"I'm going on a date, sweetheart," Morgan told her. "Rosie is babysitting you tonight."

"Oh. Okay," Abigail said. She had never been watched by anyone else before but knew that she could have anything she wanted and that Rosie was softer than her mum. This should be easy work, she thought as her mum took her to number five.

Morgan knocked on the door. "Coming," a high-pitched voice said. There was the sound of a key in the door, then it opened. A skinny woman with glasses, ruddy skin and short dark-brown hair stood there.

"Hi, Rosie," Morgan said.

"Hi! I almost didn't recognise you, Morgan! Hi, Abigail!"

"Hi, Mrs Rosie," said Abigail sweetly, not knowing what Rosie's surname was.

"I'll be back at about ten thirty p.m., eleven o'clock at the latest. Is that all right?"

"That's absolutely fine. Come in, Abigail, dear," Rosie said. Abigail grinned mischievously and went in.

"Right, I'd best get going then. Bye!"

"You knock him dead, Morgan, love. See you later!" Rosie encouraged her, then closed the door.

Morgan called a taxi and quickly made her way downstairs. It came promptly, in less than five minutes. The traffic was extremely busy though, because it was a Saturday night. Morgan kept checking her watch, hoping she wouldn't be late.

The traffic hardly seemed to move. Drivers were beeping their horns in frustration, including the taxi driver. "Come on, what's happening here?" he said impatiently. After what felt like centuries, the traffic started moving again and they were off.

Morgan arrived at Olivio's at around seven forty p.m. Thank God, she thought. I'm not late. After paying the driver, she climbed out of the taxi carefully. Looking around, she couldn't see Jose anywhere, just an extremely dapper-looking gentleman, who was also looking around.

Wait a minute, she thought. Then, she looked at the man again. It was Jose.

He looked so handsome and pristine. Not that he didn't look good in his work clothes, but he really didn't look like the same person. Morgan managed to compose herself though and slowly walked towards him.

Jose caught sight of her. "Hi, Morgan," he said and kissed her hand.

"Ooh! Hi!" Morgan replied, giggling and blushing.

"Shall we?" Jose asked and smiled his dazzling million-dollar smile. He held the door open for Morgan.

"Thank you," she said and strutted in.

A waiter approached them after Jose had closed the door. "Good evening," he greeted them.

"Hi," Jose said. "I have a table booked under the name Jose."

"Oh yes, of course. For eight o'clock. Right this way," the waiter said and led them to a table at the corner of the room. It was quieter at that end of the restaurant, so Morgan felt immediately relaxed. At least there would be a bit more privacy as well.

They looked at the wine list and Jose asked Morgan which one she wanted. She told him and he asked the waiter for two glasses of wine. When the waiter returned with the wine, Morgan took a sip. Jose watched her for a few moments and then said to her, "You look so nice in that dress."

"Thank you," Morgan said, not sure whether he meant it or not. She was never too sure with Jose.

Jose must have sensed her uncertainty because he said, "I'm being serious, Morgan. It's the perfect dress for you." He paused. Then he said, "Why must everything be so perfect for you?"

Morgan spluttered then said exactly what she knew she must say. "Excuse me, but I think it's the other way around," she told him and her tone was quite angry. "Nothing seems to please you. I don't like the way you do things; you..."

She was going to carry on, but then she noticed he was smiling and then he started to laugh.

"I'm playing, Morgan. You know, not being serious."

Morgan really felt like remaining angry with him, but she couldn't. She looked at him and then smiled and said, "I knew you were playing, really. I just–"

"You just what?"

"I, erm..."

Jose laughed again. "You get angry easily, don't you? And you think everyone is trying to upset you. But it's not that way in reality."

Morgan listened.

"You must not get so angry and frustrated. Sometimes, I am just playing," he said. He then drank most of his glass of wine in one gulp carried on talking.

They talked some more, and as they talked Morgan began to realise that Jose was not really trying to upset her or make her angry when he was doing the little things he did. He was just doing it for the fun of it. It gave him a sense of satisfaction. And whether she wanted to get all angry and upset over it was her decision.

She also felt like something was starting to change. Something inside of her that she had no control over. First, she felt butterflies. Such a light, fluttery feeling inside in her belly that made her feel like flying. Then, she started to feel more like his equal, not like someone he just ordered around. She also felt like she really had a chance with him as well.

And she knew he was not just trying to fool her into thinking she had a chance. Although he was obviously a bit playful, he was not a joker. Morgan had known him long enough to re-alise that. And although he knew he had the power to make her feel small, he only seemed to do it because he knew he had it within him. He really knew himself and that he could just do it and get away with it and taunt her and tease her. And it was strange, but this made her like him even more.

The time at the restaurant passed so quickly. Almost two hours had gone when Morgan said, "Oh my gosh! I never real-ised it was that late."

"Do you need to go yet?" Jose asked.

"Well, not just yet but soon, yes."

"All right," Jose said and called the waiter and asked for the bill. He paid for everything. Morgan suggested paying for half whilst he paid for the other half, but he was having none of it. After Jose had paid, he turned and looked at her.

"What?" Morgan asked, a bit worried, because he had his stern expression on again. "You said you were all right with paying."

Jose's expression changed again. He smiled cheekily. The smile said, "I can play with you and I'll be nice, but if you let me I will pick you up and put down and you won't know what's happened." Then he laughed a little and touched her gently on her arm.

"Come with me and we will go for a walk," Jose said and walked his amazingly confident walk. Morgan was worrying about inconveniencing the babysitter, but she just wanted to spend a bit more time with Jose and enjoy the night, so she followed him out of the restaurant.

It was winter now and the Christmas lights were on. They walked arm in arm and chatted, Jose glancing at Morgan every now and again. She felt so at ease with him and had forgotten all the bad things she had seen in him and had started to see the good things. And it felt better when she did that. She couldn't be so critical and bitter towards him anymore because it was no good for her.

They walked for a few more minutes, then Jose stopped to ask Morgan something. "Morgan," he said, "would you like to come to my house, tonight?"

She half wanted to. The other half of her knew she couldn't, though, because she was not necessarily late to pick up Abigail from Rosie's, but she had said she would be back to pick her up by ten thirty p.m., eleven p.m. at the latest. It was now 10.05 p.m., and it took about twenty minutes to get from the city centre to her area.

For a split second, Morgan actually considered ringing Rosie and telling her that she was going to be a while longer than she had originally said. She was considering going to Jose's house, but she knew she shouldn't. Not straight after the first date. Never mind the fact that she had known him for a long time. It was too soon. She knew exactly what would happen if she did as well.

"I'm sorry, but I have to get back to pick my daughter up from the babysitter," Morgan said.

"That's fine," Jose replied. "I respect your wishes. How are you getting back?"

"By taxi. There're some parked down the road."

"I will walk you," he said, his stern expression on his face again.

They walked to where the taxis were parked, and Morgan asked the driver at the front if she could get in. He said yes and asked her where she was going. After she told him, she turned to say goodbye to Jose. He kissed her – not on the lips, just a peck on the cheek. This was enough to make her blush, though, and she felt all weak at the knees.

"Bye, Morgan," Jose said with a smile then strode off.

Morgan watched him as he walked. She loved to watch him; he walked so elegantly and had a confident presence. He got smaller and smaller, then she suddenly remembered her taxi and got in. She felt a bit embarrassed and scared because the taxi driver was frowning; she saw his reflection in the mirror.

There was silence for a little bit and then the taxi driver started driving. "How did it go?" he asked suddenly.

Morgan jumped. "How did what go?" she responded stupidly.

"The date. I can see you've been on a date," he said. "I saw the gentleman walking off. I have eyes, you know. I can see, you know. Would you like to answer my question?"

Morgan couldn't believe the taxi driver. How nosey, she thought. The thought did not travel down to her mouth though. Instead, what came out was, "Very nicely, thank you."

"Good," he said. "If it hadn't gone nicely, it would have been a wasted night. And you don't want to waste time, my dear."

He went on and on as he drove. Morgan listened but not intently, because she was still thinking about Jose. She said "Hmmm" and "Yes" every now and again when the driver asked her a question but she couldn't take him seriously. She was still a bit flabbergasted that he had even asked her how her date had gone. It had gone more than very nicely, though she hadn't told him this. It had been perfect. Absolutely divine. She would remember it forever.

When the taxi reached the flats, Morgan paid the driver and thanked him. Just before she got out, he said, "Remember what I said, my dear. You don't want to waste time. And he is a nice man. Don't rush, but don't keep him waiting. Because, if you do, he will probably find someone else. Then what will you do?"

"None of your business, that's what," Morgan said, and she got out of the taxi and slammed the door shut. She rushed inside and went to flat five. Knocking on the door, she shook her head in disbelief that the taxi driver could be such a nosey parker.

She heard footsteps and then the door unlocked.

"Hi," Morgan said as soon as the door opened, then she noticed that Rosie looked a bit tense and stressed. "What's wrong? Rosie? Is Abigail all right?" she asked, concerned.

"Oh yes," Rosie said and laughed a polite but fake laugh then went on explaining that although Abigail was all right, she was not sure if she could babysit her again.

"Why's that? I realise that it's a bit after ten thirty p.m., but–"

"Oh no, it's not that, so much."

So much? So, it could have been that, but there was more.

"Your daughter is delightful, Morgan. But why is she throwing tantrums because I don't have chocolate chip cookies?"

"Because they're her favourite biscuit," Morgan explained, as though Rosie were daft. She did come across that way sometimes, a bit daft and silly and didn't really seem to understand certain things, but Morgan was a bit surprised that Abigail had even had a tantrum and didn't want it to be true. She knew it could be though and that Abigail had become spoilt. She thought Rosie would have been able to handle a challenging situation. Rosie was clearly upset and almost in tears but then snapped when Morgan explained that she thought she would have done better.

"How dare you, madam! I am not responsible for your daughter being a spoilt, difficult little brat," she said rather nastily with a condescending, frosty look on her face.

Morgan just looked her up and down and said, "Listen, it was nice of you to babysit Abigail, but you don't know what you're doing and I don't like what you said. You've just got no idea how to deal with people. There's nothing wrong with my Abigail. And before you say anyone else is a spoilt brat, take a good look at yourself. Because you're so selfish and pathetic it's unbelievable."

"Oh, why did you say that?" Rosie said, even more upset, but Morgan just called for Abigail to come out and walked back to her flat with the child. As she was putting her key in the door, she was sure she heard Rosie say something else. Morgan could hardly understand what Rosie said though, because Rosie was crying at this point, trying to tell Morgan off through tears but getting nowhere. Morgan just opened the door to her flat and took Abigail inside before slamming the door behind her and locking it.

She folded her arms and looked at Abigail. She did not smile. Abigail wondered why and asked, "Mummy, how come you're looking at me all cross?"

"Because I am cross! You're not supposed to throw a tantrum because you didn't get what you wanted. You've made me look really bad, Abigail. She thinks I haven't brought you up properly."

Abigail ran to the armchair and sat on it. She screwed her face up and folded her arms, just like Mummy.

"You said I could have what I want though, Mum. And I don't like the way she had no cookies for me. She's a nasty woman. And if she won't give me what I want, I don't want to go to her house again no more anyway, thank you."

Her little arms were still tightly folded, but Morgan's arms had unfolded, and she realised this was mostly her fault and that deep down Rosie was right about her daughter being spoilt. She was not going to ask her to babysit Abigail again, but she loved to go out socially and did not want to stop going out just to please Abigail.

"How about no babysitter? How about you spend more time with me?" Abigail demanded with a conceited look on her face.

"Mummy needs a social life, you know, sweetheart," Morgan explained softly, but Abigail covered her ears and ran to her room, closing the door behind her.

A few moments later, she started screaming, "Why don't you give me what I want! I'm a wonderfully lovely, nice, beautiful girl and must have what I want! Don't you realise this? You don't realise, do you? You'll NEVER realise anything until it's too late!"

Abigail went on and on. Morgan sighed. Her five-year-old was clearly becoming a bit of a handful. On the bright side, though, Morgan had seen a much nicer side to Jose. She hoped that the date they had had tonight would be the first of many dates.

The screaming stopped after a while. Thank God, I'm so tired, Morgan thought to herself and was relieved. She also thought about what a perfect romantic night she'd had and smiled. As she got ready for bed she kept thinking about Jose and how he had made her feel that night. He had made her feel wanted, special, uplifted.

Morgan said, "Goodnight, Abigail."

There was no reply, so Abigail was either asleep or still furious, but Morgan didn't want to investigate. She went into her bedroom and flopped down on the bed. She wondered what the future held for her and Jose. She felt so excited and couldn't wait to see where things led.

Chapter 10

The month of April had approached. It would soon be that time of year again – Easter. Abigail went crazy when Morgan took her to the supermarket and demanded the biggest Easter egg on display. She would only start crying if she didn't get what she wanted and Morgan didn't want that, so she said, "Yes, sweetheart, I'll buy it."

It cost over ten pounds, which Morgan thought was extortionate for an Easter egg, but they were already at the checkout now. As Morgan was putting everything into the carrier bags, Abigail asked her if they could open the Easter egg. Morgan told her she could open it as soon as they left the shop.

"Why can't we open it now?" Abigail moaned.

"Because we haven't paid for it yet, sweetheart. I'm still packing the stuff," Morgan explained patiently.

Abigail crossed her arms and stamped her foot. Then she looked at the bags that were already packed. The Easter egg was in one of them. She reached inside the bag quickly when her mother wasn't looking and fished it out to open it.

The till lady noticed immediately and said to Morgan, "Do you want to keep an eye on your daughter, madam?"

Morgan stopped and turned to see Abigail standing there with an opened Easter egg box, taking the wrapper off so she could have a bite. "What the hell do you think you're doing?" she asked Abigail.

"Eating my egg," Abigail replied impudently and opened her mouth to get ready to eat.

"No, you're not," Morgan said, grabbing the box and putting it back in the bag. "I already told you to wait until I've paid."

Abigail screamed. She wouldn't stop either. She went on and on screaming at the top of her voice that it was her Easter egg and she could eat it when she liked and that Morgan was a horrible mum. People were starting to look and Morgan felt embarrassed.

"That's enough, now," said Morgan, but Abigail got even louder and threw herself on the floor kicking her legs.

The till lady raised her eyebrows and just carried on scanning until everything had been scanned. Then she cleared her throat and said in a loud, clear voice, "That's eighty-seven pounds and twenty-three pence, please."

Morgan couldn't stop Abigail from screaming her head off, so she stuffed the rest of the shopping in her bags and paid the lady. She waited for her change and receipt and the till lady watched her in a "Yes, I'd be a bit embarrassed too" sort of way and then smiled sympathetically. Morgan thanked her and then put the packed bags in the trolley, wondering how she was going to coax Abigail to get up off the floor.

"Listen, sweetheart, you can have your egg now. But you need to get up first. And the screaming won't get you anywhere. Cut it out," Morgan told her assertively.

Abigail wouldn't stop. She was getting tired but she still kept going, making noise and kicking her legs until a man came over and said in the gentlest voice you've ever heard, "Do what Mummy says, darling. Get up off the floor. There's a good girl."

And to Morgan's astonishment, Abigail stopped screaming immediately and got up and looked up at this perfect stranger. Where had he come from? Who was he? She didn't have the foggiest. She just knew to do what he said and be a good girl.

Morgan looked down at Abigail then up at the man. He was extremely tall and big boned and wore a long grey coat over a white top and jeans. She had no idea where he had appeared from either but was overjoyed that he had and said to him, "Oh thank you, thank you, sir."

"Have a pleasant day," he replied and then walked off out of the supermarket.

"Right," Morgan said to Abigail. "Now, you can have your egg. Don't eat all of it at once, though, sweetheart."

Abigail held her hands out for the egg and grabbed it when Morgan presented her with it. "Is there something you want to say?" Morgan asked.

"Thank you, Mummy," Abigail answered her quietly.

Morgan felt so angry with her but decided to leave the telling off until they got home. She called a taxi and they left the supermarket and waited for it. After Abigail had eaten about a third of the egg, Morgan asked her to give it back to her and that she thought Abigail had eaten enough.

Abigail narrowed her eyes and turned her head to look at her mum. She opened her mouth and growled, "If you don't let me eat the rest of MY egg, you will be sorry. Believe me."

Morgan was stunned. She could hardly believe her ears. The child was becoming more and more difficult. She thought of a million things she could say but just ended up replying, "All right, sweetheart. You can eat the rest of YOUR egg." Then she laughed to herself and shook her head, trying to remember how it had come to this.

The taxi came after about fifteen minutes. Abigail had eaten her egg by then. Morgan put the bags in the boot and told Abigail to throw the Easter egg box in the bin. Abigail said she wanted to keep it. Morgan did not want another tantrum so she said Abigail could keep the box, although she wondered why on God's earth the child wanted to keep it. Children and the little things they do, she thought.

They got into the taxi. The taxi driver hardly said anything, but Morgan preferred it that way, when they weren't nosey. When they got back to Berrygate Heights, Morgan had never been so glad be back home. After paying the driver, she took the bags out of the boot. The driver helped her take them to the main entrance. She thanked him and he said, "Bye," and got back in the vehicle.

"Would you like to help me with these bags?" Morgan asked Abigail, mainly just to see what she'd say.

"No," was the reply, which was no surprise, really.

"Hmmm," Morgan said. "All right. Okay." And she picked up all six of the bags and dragged them into the building, Abigail holding her empty Easter egg box and walking in front of her.

Carrying the bags almost killed her, and as soon as they reached the flat, Morgan plonked them on the floor and unlocked the door.

Abigail ran in and did not even bother to help Morgan unpack. She went to her room and closed the door. Morgan asked her to come back out, half-believing she would, half-believing she wouldn't.

The door opened again and Abigail said, "I want to make something with my box."

"Later," Morgan told her. "When you've helped me unpack the bags."

"No, I want to—"

"You want to do as you're told. That's what you want to do. I'm not pleased with you at all. You behaved like an animal in that supermarket. Do you know how embarrassed I felt?"

Abigail looked at her. Her expression was one of confusion and utter disbelief. Why had her mum told her she could have what she wanted and then not let her have what she wanted and then not let her have it straightaway? Didn't she understand that she was responsible for her throwing the tantrum? It was not her fault, she knew that. She had been a good girl since the day she was born. And she couldn't believe she was being reprimanded like this. What did she do wrong?

The finger wagging and telling off went on for a long time. Morgan finished by stressing that if she ever went on like that again, she would never get anything she wanted again. This made Abigail cry. Just the thought of never getting anything she wanted again made her well up. Her mum paid no attention to her and started unpacking the shopping. Abigail kept crying and then suddenly wailed, "I'm not helping you unpack the bags! I'm making a house out of my box in my room by myself! I don't need your help!"

"Good," Morgan snapped and continued unpacking. "Go and do it."

Abigail added, "And it's going to be my special house, for me and me alone. Because you don't deserve anything. No house, no happiness, no nothing." Then she ran back in her room, slamming the door behind her.

It was no use asking her to come back out again, but what Abigail said made Morgan feel sad. Part of her thought it was true as well. That she didn't deserve anything good.

Another part of her thought, that's just Abigail. She says things like that when she's upset. The little devil.

And then, she thought, Abigail can't be right. I must deserve some happiness. But what makes me happy?

She tried to think about one thing in her life that made her happy while she finished the unpacking. Everything she had. She had a job. She had a beautiful little girl, but she was driving her up the wall. The only thing in her life that made her happy was Jose.

By now, she had saved enough money to have a professional childminder, because there was no chance of Rosie babysitting Abigail again. And again, Morgan needed someone to watch her. She still wanted to go out and enjoy her time with this man. It was not that she didn't love Abigail, but the child just wanted her mum all to herself and did not see how difficult and selfish she was being.

Morgan took her time and searched for a top childminder. Most of the ones she found were extremely posh-looking and in their adverts most of them stated they would only mind children of a particular age. Most of them were white as well and although Morgan got on with white people, she felt misunderstood by them sometimes, being a mixed-race woman. Also, because of the experience with Rosie, she thought that it would make more sense to find a mixed-race or black childminder. Then, they might be able to understand her child better than Rosie did, even if she was the spoilt brat that Rosie said she was.

Then she came across a childminder on the internet. She was called Joy Malosoku and she had a diploma in leadership for the Children and Young People's Workforce – Early Years (Management) QCF. Her advert stated that she was happy to show anyone who was interested in her services her certificate.

She was charging quite a bit at ninety-five pounds. Morgan looked at her picture. She had a dark complexion and perfectly plucked eyebrows. Her expression was pleasant. There was no smile, but Morgan took this as her being professional and serious. The number was on the screen. Why hesitate? Morgan thought and dialled the number.

The phone rang three times and then a voice answered. "Hello?"

"Hello. My name is Morgan and I've been looking for someone to babysit my child because I have a busy work life and need someone watch her."

"Let me introduce myself. I'm Joy Malosoku. You say you want me to watch your daughter. What is your daughter called? Are you finding it difficult to take care of her?"

Morgan had already started lying by telling Joy that she needed her help because of her busy work life, when it was more because of her romantic and social life. She had already started though, so she thought she may as well keep doing it.

"Oh no, I can take care of her and everything, but my boss is asking me to work nights at the weekends from next week forward, so I need someone to watch her, basically," Morgan fabricated.

"And what's she called? Your daughter?" Joy asked. She had an African accent and a friendly tone to her voice.

"Abigail."

"How old is Abigail?"

"Five years old. Six in September."

"Okay, Morgan. I'm willing to do this and I will show you my certificate to prove that I'm qualified in Early Years Management. First, I would like to meet up with you, though."

"Yes. Of course. When?" Morgan asked eagerly.

"Are you free tomorrow?" Joy responded promptly.

Morgan tried to remember what day that would be.

"Is it Saturday tomorrow?" she asked Joy.

"No," Joy replied patiently. "It's Sunday."

"Oh. Yes, I'm free," said Morgan, feeling a bit silly about forgetting which day it was.

"Right," Joy answered. "Would you be able to meet me at The Rose Café in the city centre at about three o'clock?"

The city centre was usually quiet on Sundays, and Morgan just wanted to meet the lady as soon as possible to find to whether she was the right person to leave her child with. She had to be absolutely sure. So, she agreed to meet the lady on Sunday at three p.m. And she would obviously have to bring Abigail with her, because she didn't want to leave her in the flat all alone. She also wanted them to meet each other to see how Abigail responded to the lady. Then she would know what to do.

"Perfect," Joy said. "I have your number now, as you rang me, and it is on my phone. So, I will ring you to make sure that you can still come tomorrow. Okay?"

"That's okay, yes," Morgan replied. She was glad that it was all decided.

"I will see you tomorrow then, Morgan," Joy said.

"Bye!" Morgan said chirpily and then ended the call.

Sunday came and so did the rain. Damn, Morgan thought. I hope it clears up by the afternoon.

The time was ten thirty a.m. and Abigail was still asleep. Morgan's phone rang. She picked it up hastily and answered.

"Hello?"

"Hello, Morgan, this is Joy speaking."

"How are you, Joy?" Morgan replied.

"Good, and I hope you are also well. Do you still want to meet me today? The weather is bad, so I understand if you can't–"

"Oh, no! Of course. And I'll bring Abigail with me. And we'll have a coffee and a chat."

"That is perfect. I will meet you at three o'clock in The Rose Cafe. See you later."

"See you later on, bye," Morgan said. After the call, she got a shower and got dressed. She thought Abigail was still asleep and opened the door ever so gently to come in. She was wide awake, though, holding on tightly to her teddy. Morgan looked at the little house she had made out of the Easter egg box. The cardboard was painted bright pink with little red curtains and had been cut first and then taped together. Morgan looked back at Abigail.

"Well, that's a nice house you've made."

No reply.

"How long did it take you?"

No reply.

"Are you going to be like that all day?"

Abigail hummed a tune and acted like she couldn't hear anything.

"We're going out today, you know. And you've got to be ready by one thirty p.m. so we can leave to get the bus."

"But I want to stay in!" Abigail moaned.

"Why?"

"Because it's raining!"

Morgan sighed. "Abigail, I know the weather isn't nice, but this is very important. I want you to meet someone."

Abigail turned her head to look at her mum. Oh, she wants to take me to meet a new person, she thought to herself. I wonder who it is? It must be better than staying in here, though.

"Will I get a treat if I come?" Abigail asked in her sweetest voice.

"Yes, sweetheart. Anything you want."

Abigail smiled. Ha, ha, ha, she thought. I've got Mummy right where I want her. She got washed and dressed after breakfast, just like her mum told her, and played with her toys until it was time to leave. She put on her pink wellies and purple raincoat then took her mum's hand as they left the flat.

At the bus stop, they stood under Morgan's gigantic umbrella. The rain fell heavily, and Abigail reminded herself of the treat she would get and tried not to focus on the terrible weather. She knew she deserved a treat at the very least for being put through this. A child of her age should not have to leave the comfort of indoors for any reason to be stood out on the road with that woman who called herself her mum in the rain, when they should be in with their toys and the TV and everything their way. Morgan was sick of the rain but was not going to go back to the flat. The bus was due in ten minutes. Abigail kept asking when it was coming, and Morgan would reply that it would come any minute. The child was so impatient. Morgan was finding it more difficult to cope with her every day.

When the bus came, Abigail hopped on, and Morgan climbed on after her. "Stay with me," she said.

Abigail started running upstairs. Morgan paid the fare quickly and told Abigail off for disobeying. Abigail paid no attention and wiped the condensation from the window so she could see out of it. Morgan rolled her eyes and hoped to God that Abigail would grow out of all this.

They arrived at the Rose Cafe bang on time. Morgan looked around for Joy. A woman was sat at a table in the middle of the café, waiting patiently. She looked like the woman from the photo Morgan had seen on the internet. So, she held Abigail's hand tightly and led her over to the table.

Joy saw them approaching and smiled. "Hello," she greeted them, standing up. "You must be Morgan. And you're Abigail, aren't you?"

"Yes!" Abigail exclaimed.

"Hi, Abigail, I'm Joy. How are you this afternoon?"

"I'm very, very, very grumpy about the rain. But I'm very, very, very happy to meet a new person today. Because I'm tired of her," Abigail said, but she watched the lady and wondered who she thought she was. She wondered who all these grown-ups thought they were. They couldn't do anything to her, and it would be Abigail's way or the highway.

"Tired of Mummy? Never be tired of Mummy, Abigail. Never," Joy replied.

Mmm, Abigail thought. So, you're intelligent enough to say good things in front of Mummy. You seem nice as well. I wonder why you want to set such a good impression to my Mummy by saying that?

Joy bought coffee for herself and Morgan and they talked. Morgan knew after about fifteen minutes that Joy was the person she wanted to look after her child. She was responsible, sensitive, very assertive but also had that gentle way that was necessary when looking after children. Abigail smiled and answered enthusiastically when Joy asked her a question and seemed to like her.

After Morgan had seen the certificate Joy had brought with her to prove she was qualified, she nodded and said that she was happy to pay her to babysit Abigail. As soon as she told Joy this, Abigail's facial expression turned from one of blissful happiness to one of utter misery. What? This was what her mum had taken her out in the rain for? To meet the new babysitter?

It had all been decided now though. "I'll see you soon, Abigail," Joy said pleasantly. "Bye bye."

Abigail smiled and waved but stayed quiet. Then, as soon as Joy had left the café, she turned to her mum and asked her, "Why have you done this?"

"Done what, Abigail?"

"I don't like the way you did that. I don't want a babysitter. It's not fair," Abigail complained and started crying.

Morgan bought her a cookie for her treat, but Abigail wouldn't eat it. She couldn't see why her mum couldn't be with her all the time and give her all the attention and love in the world. She threw the cookie on the floor and stamped on it. Then she ran out of the cafe. Morgan panicked and ran after her, calling her name.

She caught up with her and grabbed her hand. Abigail tried to break free and even bit Morgan, but Morgan gripped the child's hand even tighter. Then she hugged her and said it was okay if she didn't want the cookie. Abigail was still crying. Morgan didn't know what the child wanted.

Although she loved her daughter, she really was at the end of her tether. All she wanted was some happiness and to get to know Jose better. She was not going to change her mind about the babysitting agreement. She needed to keep seeing him. She needed that feeling that he gave her. She couldn't do without him.

Morgan called Joy almost every weekend to babysit Abigail. She went on date after date with Jose and every time she did, he would ask her if she wanted to go to his house. And every time she would say no. Even though she was dying to say yes.

Whenever she got home, she would feel silly for worrying, because everything had gone fine. Joy was good with Abigail because she knew she was the one in control, despite what Abigail obviously believed. Abigail respected her for this and could hardly wait to see Joy when she came around to babysit. Joy was an absolute Godsend and Morgan felt lucky that she had such a reliable, trustworthy babysitter.

It had come to the night of Morgan and Jose's fifth date. She had always shied away when he had asked her to come around to his house. Tonight, though, she couldn't hold back any more. The question came again.

"So, Morgan, would you like to come over to my house tonight?" Jose asked her expectantly, as he always did.

Morgan took a deep breath. She was ready. "Yes," she replied. "I would love to." She was so enthralled that she gave in to Jose's charms.

A smile crossed Jose's face. It was a smile that made Morgan smile. It was a smile that said, finally you have made your decision. And it's the right one.

They walked to the car park where Jose had parked. He opened the door for Morgan to get in. She climbed in cautiously and waited for him to go around the other side. He got in the driver's seat, glanced at her momentarily then started the car and left the car park.

Hardly anything was said on the way to Jose's house. He asked Morgan if she had enjoyed the meal. She said she had but it had not been what she had really wanted. And that was it.

Although they hardly said anything to each other, the atmosphere was not awkward. Both felt completely at ease in the other's company. It felt so natural, like it was meant to be, like nothing else mattered but that moment.

When they got out of the car, Jose led Morgan a few yards down the path to a huge house. It was almost like a mansion. The garden had a beautiful fountain, and there were white stones around the edges of the grass and two little trees. One was a blossom tree and the other was a sycamore tree. Morgan gasped.

Everything about this place was so enchanting that she felt like she was in a fairy tale.

They walked up the gravel path, the stones crunching under their feet. Jose got his key out of his pocket and unlocked the big mahogany front door. He pushed it open and motioned for Morgan to come in.

Before she came in, she stood momentarily on the doorstep, hardly daring to look inside. Jose noticed and touched her arm gently. "Morgan, I'm not going to hurt you. Don't worry. It's just you and me now."

Morgan felt terrified but looked inside. The vast hallway had a marble floor with a winding staircase. There were five pegs on the wall, three occupied with coats and jackets. A big black umbrella was propped against the wall near the coats. Not a speck of dirt could be seen on the floor, the wall, anywhere.

This scared Morgan even more, the spotlessness, the perfection. She couldn't stand on the doorstep all night, though. And the man standing beside her had something about him. His presence made her feel safe. She looked for something to show her that he was a bad person, that he was not really for her, but she couldn't find it.

Slowly, she stepped into the hallway, wiping her feet. Nervously, she moved near to the wall, wondering what do next. He had closed the door and locked it.

She was looking at him. He was looking at her. It was a look that made her feel vulnerable, like he could see right into her soul. Like he knew every little part of her. Like there was no escape.

And she didn't want to escape from him. When he asked her to take her shoes off and leave them in the hallway, she did so. He did the same.

"Come this way," Jose said in his calm, confident, unflappable voice and she followed obediently. They entered a room, a scarily massive room, with a cream leather sofa and a black rug on the floor. There was also a glass table and a mantelpiece with three pictures on it.

Morgan looked around, taking it all in. Again, there was no mess no clutter; it was so perfect. Then she noticed the TV in the corner.

"We're not watching TV," Jose said straight away, the moment she looked at it.

"No, it's all right. I don't want to."

"Good," he said and walked over to a glass cabinet. As he got a bottle of red wine out, he asked her, "Why don't you sit down? Make yourself at home."

Morgan shook her head, realising she was still stood in the same spot. She walked over to the sofa, not looking at him but at the mantelpiece and the clock on the wall. Then she looked at her feet shyly as he came to sit beside her. He put two glasses on the table and poured some wine. Then he watched her as she picked up her glass of wine and sipped from it.

"Mmm," Morgan said, "it's nice. Tastes fruity. It's really nice."

"I knew you'd like it," Jose replied, smiling at her.

The room went silent for a little bit. Morgan drank all her wine and then asked Jose, "What do you think of me?"

He did not hesitate to tell her straight. "What do I think? That you have a ridiculously over-confident attitude. Deep down though, I can see you're not that confident in reality."

Morgan looked a bit stunned but listened with fascination.

"I know it's just an act," he went on. "I know that you want me."

He gently started stroking her hair. Her heart started beating very fast. He looked into her eyes, his gaze steady and unflinching. "You've wanted me for a long time, haven't you, Morgan?" he whispered. "You don't have to pretend. You don't have to feel afraid. Don't be shy."

Morgan couldn't hide her feelings any longer. She couldn't hold back. Grabbing his face with both hands, she moved closer to him, and they kissed passionately. It felt so intense, so natural, so good.

After a few minutes, they managed to take a breath.

"Shall we, er," Morgan said, laughing a little, "shall we take this any further?"

"If you would like to, Morgan," Jose replied. Morgan had never anticipated that she would ever be in Jose's house, kissing him, but she felt so at ease with him that she couldn't say no. She got up and took him by the hand then softly whispered in his ear, "You know I'd like to."

They kissed again, unable to keep their hands off each other. Jose went upstairs as Morgan held onto him and followed him. There were so many stairs to climb up and Morgan felt like it was taking forever.

The moment they entered Jose's bedroom, the kissing started again. Morgan felt the warmth in her chest as they kissed, Jose's hands touching her shoulders, arms, waist, legs. They undressed each other rapidly, hardly able to control themselves. Jose held her and caressed her gently. Then, they lay down on the bed and made love. Their bodies moved in time with each other, responding to every touch the other one made. Morgan felt like she was in heaven; the feeling he gave her was simply out of this world. They went on until they were worn out then lay in bed, Jose resting his hand gently on Morgan's waist. Gazing into his eyes, she knew this was love. It felt like she didn't need to pretend; her guard had come down and she was totally free. She could be herself with him and nothing felt better than that.

Whilst they were lying in bed, Morgan's phone rang. She wrapped the duvet round her and got her phone out of her bag. Jose laid there, smiling broadly at her. He had finally won her heart.

Morgan smiled back at him and answered the phone. It was Joy. "Where are you?" she asked Morgan. "You should have been back twenty minutes ago!"

"I'm so sorry," Morgan apologised. "I-I just lost track of time."

"What are you doing?" Joy asked nosily. Jose had got out of the bed, pulled the duvet off Morgan, smiled at her mischievously and pinched her bottom. She had to restrain herself from laughing and told the childminder with great difficulty that she would be back within the hour. She ended the call and she and Jose cracked up laughing.

They put their clothes back on and went downstairs. Jose offered to drive Morgan to Berrygate Heights, and they walked out the door. Closing the door and locking it, Jose followed

Morgan down the gravel path. He cheekily looked at her rear and the sexy way she walked.

When they reached Berrygate Heights, Morgan gave him a sweet smile. "Thank you for an unforgettable night," she told him.

"Take care, Morgan," Jose replied in his cool, unflappable voice. "Bye."

"Bye!" she said then got out of the car and waved at him before running to the entrance of Berrygate Heights. She rushed up the stairs and unlocked the door to the flat. When she got in, Joy walked up to her, giving her the spare key. She didn't look very pleased but said to Morgan, "So, how was the date?"

"Oh," Morgan replied, "it was, you know... all right."

"All right?"

"When I say all right, I mean it was out of this world."

"Well," Joy replied, "I'm glad someone had a good night."

Then she started grumbling about being inconvenienced. Morgan nodded patiently and listened but said that she had paid her and that she shouldn't complain and that she was allowed to have a good time with her friend. Joy said that was okay but not to do this again. Then she got her stuff, bid Morgan goodbye and went.

Abigail woke when the door slammed. She ran to her mum, looking up at her excitedly. "How was your date, Mummy? Did you kiss?"

"Go back to bed, Abigail," Morgan said but smiled when Abigail left the room. What a night it had been! She hadn't had a night like that – well, ever. As she stood at the window and looked out, she knew that nothing would be the same between her and Jose again. They had gone from hating each other to hardly being able to take their eyes or hands off each other. What they had was special, a closeness that was so pure and mutually desired by both of them that no-one could tear them apart.

Chapter 11

It was the day after Morgan had spent the night with Jose. She felt so different, so full of energy and life. He was the one, she was sure about that. The man made her want to do crazy things. He filled her with such an unexplainable magical feeling, and she couldn't take her mind off him.

She didn't want to think about him all day, though. The weather was nice as well, so when Abigail woke up, Morgan got her ready and they went out.

On the bus, Abigail kept asking Morgan what she had been doing the night before, who she had been with, why she was acting so weird. She seemed to be in a dreamworld, and Abigail couldn't work out why. Every time she asked her mum a question, she would just get the same response: "I'll tell you later, sweetheart."

They got into the city centre soon enough, despite there being a short delay. The traffic was moving a bit slower than usual due to some kind of accident. Morgan hardly noticed though; nothing had bothered her recently. It felt like everything had finally worked out for her.

Abigail wouldn't shut up when they got off the bus. In every single shop they went in, she asked her mum for everything she saw. Morgan would usually feel annoyed with her and not bother to listen, but today she was in the best mood ever. She bought Abigail four presents and treated her to a Happy Meal. Whilst they were eating, Morgan warned Abigail that she wouldn't be getting this many presents again, not in one go, anyway. She was watching how spoilt Abigail was becoming and she didn't want things to get worse than they already were.

No sooner had Abigail and Morgan got home than Abigail was diving into the shopping bag. She pulled two Barbie dolls out as well as a Ken doll, but left the raggy doll in the bag. Morgan asked her why she had left it in.

"It's not that I don't like it... I just want to play with it later," Abigail fabricated. She didn't really like to play with raggy dolls; she had only bought it because it looked like her. It was the first toy she had picked, which Morgan was glad about. She could see that having a black childminder for Abigail hadn't exactly had a bad effect on her, but she wasn't sure whether she really liked it or not.

Abigail stayed in her room for a long time, talking in three different voices, playing as children play, pretending the toys were real people. Morgan wondered how long she would stay in there for. She made some tea and sat down to watch the TV.

After an hour or so, Abigail came out of the room and got the raggy doll out of the bag. She went back into her room, and Morgan listened carefully to what she was saying. This time, she wasn't pretending the raggy doll was real or giving it a voice, but she spoke to it very sweetly, saying, "I love you so much; you're my bestest friend. You're so pretty and I'm not going to let you come to any harm."

She sounded a lot more content now. Morgan hoped to God the contentment would last. Jose crossed her mind. She thought about last night and giggled. Then she decided to ring him.

The phone rang several times, but he didn't answer. She assumed he was busy and left a message saying how much last night had meant to her. Tomorrow, she would see him again. And she couldn't wait.

Monday came. Morgan dropped Abigail off at school. The weather was still warm, and the same feeling Jose had given Morgan hadn't disappeared. In fact, it seemed to get more and more intense as she got closer to the cafe. She felt like she was going to explode, the emotions she felt were so strong.

Jose was there when Morgan came in, behind the plastic cabinet where most of the food was. He didn't seem to realise she was there, but he was there, talking to one of the workers, so Morgan just went to the back to put her stuff in the staffroom. She put her apron on and smiled excitedly as she came back out.

As soon as she saw him, she remembered Saturday night at his house. The feeling tingled inside of her again, that beautifully light inexplicable feeling that terrified her but made her feel like the only woman in the room, like the only woman he had eyes for, like the only woman he had ever loved.

Morgan blinked, cleared her throat and said to Jose, "Hi! Did you get my message?"

To her amazement and utter embarrassment all he said was, "What message? Get on with your work!" Then he frowned at her and made her feel so ridiculously small that she almost cried. He walked away with some dirty mugs in his hand, while she stood there, feeling completely alone.

Morgan was starting to feel a bit confused now as well. She also felt hurt, because the night they had spent together had been such a wonderful, unforgettable night. He didn't seem to care.

They did not talk for the rest of the morning. Morgan was dying to yell all kinds of nasty things at him, but she just didn't have the heart to. She could see that Jose didn't want to talk to her, that he wanted it that way. It wasn't good to disrespect his wishes either, she knew that. Because he still had that control over her, that power, that ability to make her feel like she was nothing.

At midday, he approached and told her very quietly that she could go on her break. He still had a frown on his face as he walked away again. Feeling defeated in her attempt to make him love her, Morgan shook her head and went out of the cafe.

She walked slowly to the newsagents. As she walked, she thought of how foolish she had been. How could she have done this to herself? She had given herself to Jose only to be put down once again. He would never love her as much as she loved him. She had worn her heart on her sleeve and expected him not to break it, but it had happened anyway. And it was her fault for falling in love with someone like him, someone she would never truly know.

He was such a mystery. It was impossible to work him out and she didn't really want to waste any more time trying to. She didn't really want to be in the same room as him right now, so after she had bought her crisps from the newsagent's, she came out and ate them in the street.

Usually Morgan would eat in the staffroom, but she couldn't go into the cafe. She would see Jose and probably do something she would regret. She would punch him or embarrass herself in some way or another.

What she did next was very sneaky, but she remembered that he always left the back door open until the cafe closed and went around to the back. She snuck in through the back door. There was no-one else in the staffroom, luckily, but she couldn't chance anyone bursting in and seeing her. As quickly as she could, Morgan got her stuff and rushed back out before anyone saw her.

She began to walk back home. It wasn't just the way Jose had spoken to her that upset her, it was the fact that he hadn't even remembered to check his messages. She understood that he had work to do, but she couldn't believe he could be so forgetful.

That was how she felt, anyway. Like it was not important to listen to one message from someone who couldn't stop thinking about him. Like he had forgotten who she was. Like she was a stranger to him.

It was starting to get cold now. The wind blew harshly and stung her cheeks. She walked a bit faster to keep warm but wished she had stayed in the cafe.

How could she though? He had succeeded in doing the very thing she believed he would never do again. She had thought that sleeping with him would change everything. Very little had changed, though.

Morgan felt so mad at Jose, but even more mad at herself. She couldn't face him. Ever. She had given him what he wanted and couldn't undo the mistake she had made, but she knew she couldn't go back in there again.

When she got home, she locked the door and put the keys on the kitchen table. As she sat down, she realised that leaving Jose's cafe before the end of the shift was an even bigger mistake than sleeping with him. She couldn't look at her mobile phone, though, even when she felt it vibrating in her bag. He wouldn't be worrying about her necessarily, just wondering where she'd gone and angry that she hadn't even finished her shift. He only wanted her there so he could boss her around and give her endless orders.

She thought of how deceptive he had been and how she had let him charm his way into her pants. She welled up with tears. Why she was crying she didn't even know, but she couldn't stop. She had had such a beautiful night with him, but that was all it had been. One night. It would probably never happen again.

So why had she let herself get fooled like this? Why had she believed it would be a lasting relationship? Why had she let it happen only to be rejected again?

She hated the way he treated her. She hated him for doing this to her. She never wanted to work or even set foot in that cafe again.

Before Morgan knew it, half the day had gone by and it was almost time to pick Abigail up from school. She set off and tried to forget about that night, that man who had wined her and dined her and then tossed her aside. The more she tried to forget it all though, the more it played on her mind.

She collected Abigail but hardly spoke to her. The child pulled at her hand, showing her what she had made in art class. Morgan hardly noticed and just made a comment about being a bit sick of her.

Abigail let go and walked a bit more slowly. Then she crossed her arms, scrunching her face up.

"I'm not talking to you," she moaned. "And you know why? Because you're not listening to me. And it's my painting, so booyakasha!"

"Just shut up, Abigail," Morgan snapped angrily.

Abigail went on and on about the painting that she had done, on her own, and how she was proud of it and that she really wanted Morgan to see it. Morgan knew that Abigail was just showing off, but eventually she had to listen and look, even though she was sick of her life and felt like dying.

The painting was not what she had expected it to be. She expected it to be of a butterfly or a rainbow, but it was of two people who were holding hands with a child. Abigail watched Morgan as she looked at it, and she didn't smile, but she said, "Do you know who it's of, Mummy?"

"No," Morgan told her, but she was just playing like she didn't know. "It's a beautiful painting, sweetheart. What I'll do is I'll put it on the fridge when we get home."

Morgan knew what her daughter was trying to say to her. All she wanted was a proper family with a mummy and daddy. She was really sick of having to be mummy and daddy for Abigail. Her child could be so difficult. Did she expect her mummy to just buy her a daddy at the shop? Morgan loved Abigail but she felt so angry with her sometimes.

They got home and the first thing that Morgan did was put the little painting on the fridge with a little magnet. Abigail was delighted when she did that. She hadn't really noticed or thought of the reason why Mummy wasn't talking much on the bus. She wasn't talking much now, but she smiled at Abigail and told her to go and play in her room.

Morgan was disappointed in herself and realised that she had made a big mistake by walking out. Suddenly, she ran to the bag she had dumped on the chair, which had her phone in it. Hastily she pulled it out and looked at the screen.

Then she gasped. There were five missed calls, all from Jose. There was also a message on the voicemail. She listened to it, but she didn't really like hearing that she shouldn't have gone out of the cafe without saying bye and that if she didn't ring back she would lose her job. So, she turned the phone off and started making tea.

Morgan really didn't want to think of Jose. She certainly didn't want to think about the stupid mistake she'd made by walking out of the cafe. It would just make her feel even worse. She thought about the beautiful night they'd had together. It was so special and had felt so right.

Jose had upset her so much that she couldn't even bring herself to ring him and have a big go at him. Morgan called Abigail in tears; she couldn't even set the table. Abigail asked her if she wanted her to put the knives and forks out.

"Yes, sweetheart, that would be helpful," Morgan said gratefully.

She was feeling so low that she was thankful to have such a lovely daughter even though she was the biggest bundle of trouble ever. After the table was set, Abigail got stuck in and gobbled the chilli con carne and rice up in no time. She noticed that someone opposite her wasn't eating hers though, which wasn't really like her. She looked so sad as well. Abigail had sensed something wasn't quite right as soon as her mummy had called her back in the room. Maybe it was because of something that had happened to her while she was at work. She didn't want to ask though, so she said sweetly, "You'll get better, Mummy. And I love you." Then she went to her room.

After Abigail had left the table, Morgan just sat there, staring into space. She felt so guilty, like she had let her child down. She had barely spent any time with Abigail recently and things had changed. Morgan had been more interested in spending time with a man who hadn't been as concerned for her as she had thought. She felt so mad at herself and felt that she was a failure.

She should have been there for Abigail. She knew now how selfish she'd been. Abigail was the best thing her life, and she should have put Jose and her own needs after Abigail's needs. As Morgan washed the dishes, she wondered what to do about everything.

The only thing she could think to do was escape. She didn't think; she couldn't think, not after what she had experienced that day. When the dishes were washed, she left the flat to clear her head.

Stupidly, she forgot to lock the door. She was in a rush to get to the shops. Running down the road to the off-licence, Morgan just wanted to forget what had happened. She bought three big bottles of alcohol and left the shop.

Slowly, Morgan walked back up the road. She felt so angry with Jose. She was determined not to talk to him, text him, leave a message or give him any sign that she had forgiven him. As she entered the main entrance of the tower block, she started shouting and swearing.

She sat on the steps and opened a bottle of vodka. She drank almost all of it, but then she heard a voice. She didn't recognise the voice and dropped the bottle, startled.

It hit the floor and smashed into small, jagged pieces. Morgan put her hands to her face. She couldn't make sense of the situation. The voice came again.

"Mummy? Mummy, what have you been doing? Where have you been?"

Morgan got up and turned around. She saw a little brown girl with her hair in bunches. Then she saw a woman standing behind her. The woman looked a bit concerned. Morgan squinted her eyes, as she couldn't recognise her at first. It was the woman who used to babysit Abigail, Rosie.

"Is everything okay, Morgan?" Rosie asked in a tentative voice.

"NOOO!" yelled Morgan and then she started banging her head against the wall. Abigail screamed, telling her to stop, but she wouldn't. Then, Morgan collapsed on the steps and the colour went from her face.

A beeping sound woke Morgan up. She opened her eyes and saw a dazzling white light. She knew she was not in heaven, although she had thought so for a second, because what was the beeping sound?

Then she saw a man with a mask over his face, a green mask and green overalls with a green cap. Now she realised where she was. In hospital.

She remembered that she had done something really stupid but couldn't remember what it was. Suddenly, she jerked and started to panic.

"Abigail! Where is she?" she asked the doctor.

"Don't panic," the doctor said, trying to calm Morgan down. "Your daughter is all right."

Morgan didn't believe him. It took her a while to settle and even then, she couldn't think of much but her daughter. She wondered how her child was. She wondered where they'd taken her. Maybe she was with Rosie, who had found Abigail the very same day when she had made that foolish mistake of leaving her daughter in the flat alone with the door unlocked. She could never forgive herself.

What if Rosie had told Social Services? Morgan would be in trouble, and they might deem her an unfit mother. Then what would she do?

Then she remembered work. All she could think of was someone making her feel really bad the last time she went. She couldn't remember who it was. They weren't important to her. Abigail was the most important person in the world to her.

However, no-one would tell Morgan where Abigail was. This was three days after the incident. It took her a further two weeks to get back to normal before she was finally discharged from the hospital. She found out where her child was in the end. They had put her in care, because just as Morgan had thought, nosey Rosie had phoned Social Services when she saw that Morgan wasn't taking care of herself or her child.

Morgan could not for the life of her remember that she had left Abigail in the flat. Weirdly, even though they had told her that Abigail was in care, Morgan still expected her to be there when she got back. Abigail was nowhere to be seen though.

Morgan cried. Tears of confusion and self-pity rolled down her face. She fell to her knees, praying to Jesus, asking him where she'd gone, where her pretty little daughter had gone. She couldn't seem to accept that they had taken her away.

Then, she turned to look at the painting on the fridge of the three people. That was all the child had wanted. Three people, mother, father, daughter, living together in peace. A real family. Morgan stood up and went into Abigail's room.

The little house was still there – the house that Abigail had made out of the Easter egg box. Her house, she had told Morgan. All to herself. She can't have meant it, Morgan thought. All to herself? Was she talking about when she got older? Or did she just need a father figure?

Who could be her father though? Morgan couldn't think of anyone to be the child's father. And she knew one thing – she had to get her child back.

Chapter 12

Ever since the day Morgan had abruptly left the cafe, Jose had attempted to contact the woman every single day. She absolutely hated him for daring to call her. However, the messages left on her phone weren't necessarily asking her to come back: he was asking how she was and at the end of each message he always told her to take care.

Morgan knew she would have to return to work at some stage though. And the longer she put it off, the harder it would be to go back. What she was dreading most of all was telling Jose that her child had been taken away from her. She wanted Abigail to come home so badly it was killing her. Abigail was the only person that mattered to her, and she couldn't trust Rosie at all now, not after what she had done. How could she get Social Services involved?

The anger was starting to eat away at her. She couldn't trust anyone either. Not even Jose. She realised she must ring him instead of fuming and wishing he wouldn't tell her to take care. Because she knew he was right, as always. So, she rang him.

"Hello?" Jose's voice came from the other side of the receiver.

"Hello, Jose? It's me, Morgan."

"I didn't think you would ever ring again," he said in his stern voice.

Morgan stayed quiet, wondering if he was angry or not, but then he kind of laughed and continued, "But I knew you would ring at some point. How is everything?"

"Er, not good, really." And she told him everything. About leaving Abigail in the flat, about getting drunk out of her senses, about the neighbour calling Social Services and about being in hospital because the neighbour hadn't been that bad really, she had come to realise. At least she had recognised that someone wasn't well and called a bloody ambulance for them. Morgan felt a little bit bad about being ungrateful towards Rosie and Jose could hear it in her voice; he could tell.

"Well, you should be more grateful, yes. And thank somebody, you know. Quickly!"

"I'll thank God, but I don't really want to thank her for anything," Morgan told him. There was a little silence that lasted a few seconds. "Hello?" Morgan said. "Are you there?"

"Mmmm. I'm just thinking," Jose said. "Thinking of whether to give you a second chance."

Morgan thought he was talking about the relationship at first and got a little tense. To her surprise though, all he said was that she could keep her job and that he would help her as much as he could. He let her know one thing – he didn't really like the way she had walked off that day. He asked her why she had done it.

She wouldn't tell him. All she had to say was, "Sorry, Jose. I'll be in tomorrow. See you."

At work the next day, it felt to Morgan as if she had never been gone. Jose stayed out of her way and watched her out of the corner of his eye, monitoring her, but she didn't care. She was just there to do her job now. How else could she survive?

They had taken Abigail away and it was all her stupid fault. The only way she could get her back was with Jose's help. She knew what he could be like sometimes though. Stubborn. The cafe was his main priority, to keep the business going.

Somehow, she had to persuade him to ring the care home. She flirted with him a little and he seemed a bit irritated, but she persisted and asked him for a favour. He was astounded, and it took a lot of persuasion, but he actually agreed to ring them.

And he did. Morgan got back to work, believing everything was sorted. Jose knew better than to tell them everything Morgan wanted him to, though, and he didn't do a thing to convince them she was well enough to take her daughter home.

Instead, he was extremely honest. "She has solely been focusing on her work and her needs. I think she is decent enough to think of her daughter and to keep going for her. But I'm not going to help her that much. Because she hasn't been very responsive when I talk to her."

After Jose had ended the call, he went back to work. Morgan asked him if he'd spoken to the care home. He nodded and smiled, then he turned and went back to the cafe. Morgan noticed he was a bit quiet, which was not like him. "Oh no," she thought. "He hasn't done it. He's taken the piss and then thought it was funny. He hasn't convinced them I'm well enough to look after Abigail."

Then Morgan told herself to think positively and kept working, having no doubt in her mind that everything would get back to normal.

Five weeks later, Morgan got a call from the care home. They informed her that Abigail was not there. Morgan panicked, worried that they had done something bad to her. She asked them what they'd done.

"We haven't done anything to her," said the lady on the other side, sounding a bit offended. "Abigail is doing fine, and her foster parents are taking care of her."

Morgan couldn't make her mind up whether to take their word for it or not. After a while she said resignedly, "All right. As long as she's doing all right. I miss her, though. When I can I see her?"

"You can visit her whenever you're ready. I'll give you the address. It's 48 Hilton Place."

Once Morgan had written the address down, she thanked the lady and then went straight to the foster parents' house in a taxi. She couldn't wait to see Abigail's little face again and squeeze her cheeks.

Morgan rang the doorbell when she got there. A few moments later, someone could be seen through the glass window of the door. It was a man with fair hair, and when he opened the door he frowned and said, "Hello, can I help you?"

"Where's Abigail?" Morgan asked.

"How did you find us?" the man asked her suspiciously.

"Does it matter now I've found you?" she asked, starting to get impatient. "And in case you're wondering who I am, I'm Morgan. Abigail's mother."

A woman appeared at the door next to the man. She had thick brown hair and wore red-rimmed glasses. "Hi there. May I ask who you are?"

"Who do you think I am?" Morgan snapped nastily. Then she called Abigail's name. The foster parents looked at each other whilst Morgan said, "Mummy's here, Abigail. Come out, come out, wherever you are."

The woman said to the man, "What are we going to do?"

The man looked at Morgan and slowly opened the door, calling Abigail downstairs. Then he said, his eyes widening a little, "It's Morgan, isn't it?"

"Yes, it is," Morgan said assertively. "And I've come for my little girl."

He let her in. Abigail was stood at the foot of the stairs. In her hands, she held a little pink teddy bear that Morgan did not recognise. When she saw her mum standing in the doorway, she threw the toy on the floor and ran towards her mum, her arms wide open, and they hugged.

Morgan must have apologised to her a million times and said she would never leave her on her own again and that she was all that mattered to her.

Abigail picked up the toy. The man and woman introduced themselves to Morgan – the man was called Bill and the woman was called Angela. Then they all went in the living room, sat down and talked things over.

"So," the man started to say, "what do we think is the best course of action to take?"

"Well, Bill," Morgan said, clearing her throat, "I'm being honest here when I say I think you've done a great job looking after my girl."

She hesitated then enthusiastically pleaded, "But she's my daughter! She belongs with me! Oh, I love my little Abigail!" And she squeezed the life out of the child again.

Bill smiled, then he asked, "What do you want to do, Abigail?"

"I want to go home with Mummy," Abigail admitted but not ashamedly.

"I agree," Bill said. "What about you, Angela?"

Bill's partner looked up and agreed as well. "Yes, that will be the best thing for Abigail, I think."

Abigail and Morgan got Abigail's possessions and put them in bags. Then they bid Bill and Angela farewell and waited for the taxi to come. The ride was long, and Abigail didn't say much, which Morgan couldn't understand.

It wasn't the same when they got home. Abigail kept playing with the pink toy her foster parents had given her and forgot about her other toys given to her by her mum. Plus, she gave Morgan even more lip than before.

She kept asking when they would get the dream house she had always wanted. She also asked when she would have a daddy who loved her. She wanted to know why she couldn't have a real family like the other children at school with a mummy AND a daddy.

Morgan couldn't answer any of her questions. Jose came into her head all of a sudden. She knew that he wasn't exactly the nicest person when he was ready. It couldn't hurt to introduce them to each other though. He had a good nature. He had never cut off from Morgan. He could be the father Abigail had always wanted.

For some bizarre reason, Morgan never could forget the way he had made her feel when she asked him about the message she had sent him. She still felt angry and bitter towards him sometimes. It wasn't about how she felt though. It was about how Abigail felt. Her needs. And she was on good terms with Jose. What did she have to lose?

Chapter 13

A few weeks had passed since Morgan had brought Abigail home. It was a sunny afternoon and Morgan told Abigail they were going to the park. Abigail had calmed down a bit and was used to being at home again and amiably agreed to go for a walk.

There were a lot of people there, people walking dogs, cycling, jogging, people having picnics and feeding the ducks in the lake, old couples taking afternoon strolls. Morgan walked with Abigail down to the bottom end of the park, where most of the benches were. There was a tall man, thin as a rake with dark hair, sitting on the one in the middle. When he saw Morgan, he stood up.

Abigail had never seen him before and wondered who he was. He hugged Morgan and then said to Abigail with a friendly smile, "Hi. You must be Abigail. I'm Jose, your mummy's friend."

"Do you work with Mummy?" Abigail asked.

"Yes, I do," Jose replied. "How did you know?"

Abigail just smiled and all at once seemed ever so shy, which surprised Morgan. This was not Abigail's nature, but children were so funny and changeable sometimes. Morgan, Jose and Abigail strolled round the park. As Morgan and Jose talked, Abigail chipped in every now and again, saying things like, "I'm still here, you know," and "Are you Mummy's boyfriend?" to Jose.

Jose laughed and told her they were just friends, but he wasn't fooling the child. Abigail knew Jose and her mum fancied each other. She thought Jose talked a bit differently to the locals and that he was a bit mysterious, but she liked him. This was because he wasn't pretending to be her friend and seemed a bit stone-faced, but he was kind and friendly.

The ice cream van pulled up and Abigail said she wanted one. Jose bought her an ice cream with a flake and sprinkles. She said "Thank you," sweetly and started eating it.

They talked a bit more, Jose and Morgan, but Abigail didn't know what they were talking about. It was grown-up stuff. Too much for her to understand. She did a little dance to get their attention but they didn't seem to notice.

"Hey!" she screamed. "Tell me what you're talking about!"

"None of your business, cheeky," Morgan told her but not in an angry way.

"Look, Abigail!" Jose said, pointing to the sky.

Abigail looked up. There was a big, beautiful rainbow in the clear blue sky. Not a single cloud could be seen. There was a flight of doves just above the trees, and a little butterfly fluttered up to Abigail and landed on her hand. Its wings were an orangey-red colour with black markings. After a few moments it flew away, and Abigail watched it before turning to her mum and saying, "When are we going home, Mummy?"

"Why? It's a nice day, no rush to get back home."

Abigail sighed. She liked Jose, but she didn't know him very well and didn't want to stay in the park with someone she had only just met. Morgan picked up on this and reluctantly gave in. "All right," she groaned. "Let's go home, then. Jose, thank you for meeting us today."

"It's fine, it's fine. I will see you soon," Jose said, giving her a relaxed smile. "Bye."

"Bye," Morgan said, and she walked one way with Abigail while Jose walked the other way.

As the weeks passed by, Jose and Morgan became very close again. One night Morgan invited him over and they all had carbonara. Then, Morgan asked Abigail to go to her room. She didn't really want to at first, but she knew that her mum was in love with Jose and that she wanted to spend some time with him. So, she went to her room and closed the door.

She could hear them chatting and laughing. After a while, she heard them walking towards her mother's room. The door opened and closed. A few minutes later, there was a moaning sound and she heard her mum's voice saying, "Yes! Yes! Yes!" and wondered what the noise was about. She had a good idea about what grown-ups did in bedrooms though and giggled to herself.

A year later, Morgan had a baby. It was a girl – she named her Violet. Abigail was so happy to have a little sister.

They were still living at Morgan's flat, but Jose was in touch with her. He had also proposed to Morgan, and she had said yes. She felt so lucky to be engaged to the man of her dreams.

They were to marry a year later, and Joy, the childminder, would sit with the children during the ceremony. Jose came to see Morgan and the two children almost every day. And they all looked forward to the day when they would all move in with each other at Jose's beautiful mansion. So, after all the hardship and struggles, Morgan had finally got everything she had ever wanted and more.

THE END

The author

Janine Lewis was born in 1989 in Leeds, where she still lives, and attended Mount St Mary's Catholic High School. Her career is currently based in retail and her interests include painting, going to the gym and, of course, writing. The Girl at the Hostel is Janine's first published work.